Leo Sabov imagined no nightmare worse than losing his wife Maria. Not until he brought her home to Transylvania to rest.

The old mother dog took a few stiff-legged steps forward, more than a dozen of her young following. Her sharp, fast barks were interrupted by low growls. Even from three floors up, Leo could see her long hair rise into hackles from her neck to the base of her tail. She walked forward again, her group in near lockstep beside her.

The shadows in the yard were deep with the sun barely over the towering, fir-covered mountain behind Leo. That had to explain the odd shape moving from behind the log and stone building below.

The inky phantom shifted, seeming to change as it moved, every sight more unsettling than the last.

A puddle of water, a deeper shadow, a slithering snake; a terrified cat, a deformed child, a staggering bear.

Leo leaned forward, drawing breath to call out to the girl walking across the dark green grass, egg basket in the crook of one arm. Whatever that thing was, his guts twisted at the thought of it being so close to her.

Until Death: Book One of the Death and Redemption Series

Copyright © 2016 by Kari A. Kilgore

All rights reserved

Published 2016 by Spiral Publishing, Ltd.
www.spiralpublishing.net

Book and cover design copyright © 2016 by Spiral Publishing, Ltd.
Cover art copyright © 2016 by Fabio Formaggio | Dreamstime.com and Csaba Peterdi | Dreamstime.com

ISBN-13: 978-0-9908875-1-5
Library of Congress Control Number: 2016915453

For letting me stay up late to watch Dark Shadows.
For constant trips to the library and bookstore.
For awesome 70s parenting that let me watch movies and read books a bit before my time.
And for always encouraging me to learn and explore and to never doubt that I **could**.

This one's for you, Mom.

UNTIL DEATH

BOOK ONE OF THE DEATH AND REDEMPTION SERIES

KARI KILGORE

SPIRAL PUBLISHING, LTD.

Chapter 1

THE VILLAGERS never paid attention to the dogs anymore.

The constant barking and scrabbling was background noise after years of so many strays learning to survive past their pampered origins. The rich, forested mountains in Transylvania were kinder than the crowded streets of Bucharest, under Communism or decades later. Creatures meant to warm laps and comfort hands have no easy transition to wandering, endlessly searching for shelter.

Some whisper of instinct surely must remain, even with every appearance of wild ancestors bred out of them decades before.

Leo Sabov wondered at that every time he was in Romania, how such a huge population could go unnoticed in the city or in the country. People could get so worked up over stray animals in the US, yet somehow the nomadic animals here seemed healthier and more content with less attention.

He sipped strong coffee on his third floor balcony, watching the first rays of sunlight trace orange fire on the sharp granite cliffs above the tree line across from him. His bare feet were pleasantly chilled by the tile, his mind soothed by his first good night of sleep in many weeks. Staying up too late and drinking too much with his little brother usually had the opposite effect.

A young girl walked through the chicken coop below, gathering eggs for the guests of the inn he'd been returning to with his wife for over twenty years. The milling birds stirred up a scent of rich earth strong enough to overcome even the coffee. The girl sang to herself, a sweet song at odds with the quarreling chickens and agitated dogs. Maria would have known the words to the song, would have whispered them into Leo's ear.

He rubbed his eyes, struck by a different sound in one of the dog's voices. His mind seized on the escape from memory. An old female with the dangling teats of many pregnancies stood in the neat yard beside the inn. She stared at something Leo couldn't see behind the rough-hewn logs of the outdoor kitchen. Her black and tan coat was healthy, and she was normally friendly, one of the sweetest in the village. This morning, though, her voice had a harsh, desperate edge.

Dogs began to gather around her, from neighboring houses and inns, from their rough shelters on the hillsides. Some looked around, searching for what was bothering her so, then resumed their normal morning discussions and investigations. The others, many of them clearly her offspring with that same rangy body and distinctive coloring, watched her silently at first. Then their voices began to take on that same worried note.

The old mother dog took a few stiff-legged steps forward, more than a dozen of her young following. Her sharp, fast barks were interrupted by low growls. Even from three floors up, Leo could see her long hair rise into hackles from her neck to the base of her tail. She walked forward again, her group in near lockstep beside her.

The shadows in the yard were deep with the sun barely over the towering, fir-covered mountain behind Leo. That had to explain the odd shape moving from behind the log and stone building below.

The inky phantom shifted, seeming to change as it moved, every sight more unsettling than the last.

A puddle of water, a deeper shadow, a slithering snake; a terrified cat, a deformed child, a staggering bear.

Leo leaned forward, drawing breath to call out to the girl walking across the dark green grass, egg basket in the crook of one arm. Whatever that thing was, his guts twisted at the thought of it being so close to her.

Before he could open his mouth, a pathetic, mange-covered dog stepped out into the sunlight beyond the kitchen. Her light brown coat missing in patches, her body desperately thin.

The group of dogs moved forward again, all of them joining with the ancient female this time, their barking fast as a machine gun. The poor stray picked up speed. She glanced at the inn, seeming to stare right into Leo's eyes, before she broke into a run toward the outskirts of the village.

Too many of the villagers had forgotten the dogs, forgotten their ancient pact to trade shelter and affection for far superior senses. The dogs remembered.

Chapter 2

Six days ago

LEO FOLLOWED THE INNKEEPER, struggling to pay attention to what Costel was saying through a haze of grief and jet lag. A tour of the inn hardly seemed necessary when he'd been coming here for nearly twenty years with his wife, even if he was here to bury her now. All he wanted was somewhere to go to sleep and try again to pretend none of this was happening, if only for a couple of hours.

"You said you may be staying with us for a couple of weeks?" Costel said for at least the second time. The lanky, bearded man towered over Leo, his blond crew cut and dark blue eyes a sharp contrast to Leo's light brown eyes and wavy brown locks brushing his shoulders. Maria would have been after him to cut a few inches off that mop on his head long before it got to this point, if she hadn't been so busy dying.

Leo blinked and forced himself to pay attention. They were in the small kitchen in the indoor dining room, mostly a place to warm food brought from the main kitchen or from the bakery in town. He and Maria had reheated leftovers and made coffee here many times, but otherwise he'd only walked by on the way to their room.

His room now.

"At least a week," Leo said. "Probably two. Maybe a little longer. Assuming you have space for me, I mean."

"Leo, of course I do. We want you here for as long as you need to be, and we'll take very good care of you." He put his hand on Leo's shoulder as he turned to a small door across from the kitchen. "I know jet lag can make for strange meal schedules, so please make yourself at home and eat as you need to. You know about the refrigerator, and we'll leave small things out for you. And please use anything in the pantry that you need."

He opened the door, barely two feet wide, onto a small space lined with shelves and jammed full of spices, dry goods, and jars of pickles. Leo flinched at the top shelves, hoping his friend didn't notice. Hot acid flooded his throat and his heart pounded. Those shelves were lined with bottles of wine, various types of whiskey and brandy, and every kind of glassware he could imagine. He'd never even noticed that door before, much less imagined something so insignificant could slam him back into a past nearly as painful as his present.

"If you need anything that's not here, please let me know and we'll get it for you," Costel said, either not noticing or ignoring Leo's upset. "Such things are never easy, but we want to do anything we can to help you."

Leo nodded as he stepped forward and closed the door with a shaking hand. He knew he'd fail miserably if he tried to explain why a damned pantry and an offer of comfort made him react as if the man had held a gun to his head.

"Thank you, Costel," he said. "I appreciate it. I'll let you know. I promise."

Costel held a hand over his heart and lowered his head for a second.

"Then if you don't need anything this evening, I'll show you to your room. You get all the rest you can. Breakfast will be ready when you are, my friend."

Leo's heart sank when he headed toward the stairs, made from varnished half-logs with a rail to match. There were only a few rooms up there, including the only room he'd ever stayed in on their many trips to Transylvania. He wasn't sure if it would be more heartbreaking to stay somewhere else or more lonely to stay here without his wife for the first time. He was about to find out.

"I've made up your same room," the innkeeper said, and he was indeed walking toward the front of the building. "If you'd rather stay somewhere else, we have a few other rooms available. I thought..."

Leo glanced up, focusing on Costel's face for the first time. The first time he'd focused on anyone's face since he'd walked out of the hospice ward for the last time just over twenty-four hours ago. Costel could be counted on for a hearty laugh and smile, tireless energy, and a warm embrace for any arrival or departure. Leo had never seen him sad or even moody.

Right now his face was twisting and tears stood against his pale eyelashes.

"It's fine, really," Leo said. "I want to stay here, in our room. She'd want that, too. Thank you."

Costel tried to smile, but his features crumpled instead. Leo stepped forward and hugged him, relieved to comfort someone else after countless hours of not being able to do that for himself. Costel took a deep breath, patted Leo's back, and stepped away. He wasn't quite smiling, but the crisis had passed.

"I will leave you then. Sleep as well as you can."

Leo took his own deep breath before he opened the wood plank door with an actual metal key, attached to a tiny log with the room number burned into it. The same miniature bathroom in the corner, the same huge wardrobe built of more of the rough-hewn logs, the same white walls and sheer white curtains over the balcony door.

He'd spent more time than he could stand to remember in this room, talking, sleeping, making love in the middle of the night, or even the middle of the day. All he could see was empty space without Maria. Without her clothes, her scent, her voice.

He crossed in a few strides, feet shuffling on the flat gray carpet, and sat down hard on the bed. His back and thighs protested at how firm that European mattress was, and he knew his hips and shoulders would take up the chorus by the time he woke. Leo held his head in his hands, exhausted and afraid he wouldn't be able to sleep. The only thing worse might be sleeping deeply enough to dream.

That pantry. Of all the things he thought he'd been prepared for, now and one year ago. What an absurd, pathetic thing to knock a man reeling, to push him out of his own shaky grasp on reality.

Chapter 3

One year ago

Leo strained in the narrow, musty space, asking himself yet again if changing the light bulb in a useless corner of their house could possibly be worth this much trouble. His calves ached from balancing on the tiny stepladder while his toes threatened to slip backwards out of beat up sandals. The ancient, dead incandescent bulb had come out easily enough. He grunted, shifting his grip on the twisty new fluorescent one in his fingers.

Maria would have said his natural stubborn had kicked in, pushing his logical mind out of the way. If she'd been home instead of hospitalized yet again, she would have said that. Boredom and loneliness without her had driven Leo into a likely losing battle with the unreasonable Los Angeles housing market already. No matter what his wife might have said, he probably should have climbed the shelves instead of trying to wedge a too-short ladder back here.

"Brilliant idea," he whispered. "Get that light working so you can verify the builders should have boarded this up to begin with. You'll feel better about your whole damned life then."

The grooves in the base slipped into alignment with the gritty socket at last. He turned the bulb slowly, not wanting to create an even bigger project for himself by twisting the thing until it broke.

He stepped down off the ladder and flipped the switch with his elbow. Leo remembered to breathe when the dead light bulb he'd just replaced slipped out of his fingers and exploded into shrapnel all over his feet.

So many bottles, more than he could count standing here. More than he could fit into his reality. Those fucking curved green bottles. Maria hadn't even bothered to buy a different brand.

When he did breathe, it was a gasp harsh enough to tear through his throat, sharp as the frosted white glass digging between his toes, under the soles of his feet. He caught the rich, metallic scent of blood, but underneath was that bite of juniper. The perfume of those first shared drinks together, the taste of her mouth. Later the stench of her breath and skin and the taste of every part of her body at the end when she drank more than she ate.

Leo finally stepped backward, out of the blood-slicked leather, his feet slipping on the cold white-tiled floor of the kitchen. Twelve years of those blasted meetings. Drunks calling in the middle of the night. His wife getting up and leaving him cold and alone so she could rescue yet another lost soul.

Had any of it been true? There were dozens of empty bottles on the floor with a narrow path through them, maybe a hundred. Maria must have started drinking again years ago, right? She couldn't have put this many away in just a few months time.

But Leo remembered when they were in college, how she could swallow their rent money in a few days without even trying and still manage to make the Dean's list over and over again.

Her law practice had only suffered over the past couple of weeks when she was too weak and ill to go to work, but that didn't mean a damned thing. Was she in the hospital right this second getting treated for liver failure instead of some mysterious disease no one could diagnose?

He was only in this damned pantry, the useless space at the end of the laundry room, because she was finally sick enough to admit she needed help. Leo was a creature of habit, and his habit was to putter around the house when he was anxious and upset.

His main worry had been the unknown ailment that had gradually robbed her of her vitality and was starting to show in her bloated face and stomach. Stepping into this wasted space, some realtor's idea of a selling point, had thrown him into a nightmare he'd thought was in his past.

There were at least thirty full bottles on the shelves too, hidden in this awkward space neither of them used. Had she kept that dead bulb in here on purpose, just to keep him from seeing? Did she sneak in here with a flashlight, sit on that filthy stool and guzzle that shit? Then chew her endless supply of spearmint gum, what she called her sobriety crutch to avoid smoking?

Why the hell had she kept the empty bottles?

He looked down at his crimson footprints, then back at the bottles on the floor of the pantry, several coated with a thick layer of dust.

The first time it had been the blood, Maria's blood, that yanked Leo out of his cocoon of denial and forced him to deal with how deep he'd fallen into the rabbit hole with her. That just-short-of-condemned house back East, what they'd been reduced to when she drank up everything they earned at part-time jobs. Disgusting stained brown carpet, warped countertops, cheap wood paneling that never did feel clean.

His blood on white tiles that cost a fortune, imported from some-where on the other side of the planet to prove how far they'd come. Her blood on that bargain basement carpet. Hers hadn't come from glass, at least not that she'd stepped on.

Maria had tried to get away like she always did back then, pulling away from Leo when he tried to get the highball glass out of her hand. She hadn't tripped on a damned thing, at least he didn't think so now. Back then he'd tried to convince himself it was that carpet. Not only thin as a sheet but laid badly, with little wrinkles that caught every scrap of dust, food, and hair.

No, Maria hadn't tripped over anything but her own feet. Leo had watched helplessly when her head slammed into a bookcase that rebounded against the one brick wall in the whole place. For a long time after that night, before she managed to claw her way out of the thicket of juniper she'd disappeared into, he'd wondered if it would have been kinder if she'd slammed into the wall instead.

She'd sat back hard, books falling from the shelves around her legs, blood falling from her gashed forehead. She'd touched the wound, not feeling it when her fingertips brushed the blinding white bone escaping the bonds of flesh and muscle.

Twenty-seven meticulous stitches had closed the wound, but she carried a sunken scar a bit darker than the rest of her skin no matter what dermatologists tried to do about it. Sometimes she covered it with bangs, sometimes not. Maria refused more surgery, saying the scar reminded her how far down she could get.

Leo backed up against the opposite wall in their hard-won Southern California paradise. Metal handles of drawers dug into his spine one after the other as he sank to the floor, bleeding feet out in front of him. If his wife had been drinking long and hard enough to put her liver into the advanced stages of shutdown, she might have finally found a bottom neither of them could claw their way out of.

Chapter 4

Ten years ago

THE PRIVATE ROOM at the traditional Romanian restaurant in Queens was warm and cozy—and more crowded than Maria liked. The dark wood panels of the walls contrasted with the bright white ceiling that made her eyes ache in the glare of a crystal-clear May afternoon.

At least thirty middle-aged women and their adult children, most of the older generation from other parts of the world like Maria's mother and Leo's great-grandmother, crowded into the space that could comfortably seat about twenty. The remains of a rich, delectable feast—complete with lamb, pork, and chicken—had yet to be cleared to make room for what would surely be a dizzying array of pastries to go with the American-style frosted Mother's Day cake.

This had always been a difficult day for Maria, ever since she understood motherhood wouldn't be easy for her, and maybe not possible. The rough scars across her abdomen had always been a fact, part of her like her green eyes or thick brown hair. A terrible bout of appendicitis and emergency surgery had left extensive damage, including throughout her reproductive organs. The twisting white marks, and what they meant, had always been part of Maria's life. A part she never thought much about until she married Leo.

Everything else seemed normal for both of them, yet two years of trying and three rounds of IVF had failed. Something else had to be going on, and her parents had never been much for discussing the past. Especially not the past before they'd fled Romania when she'd barely started school.

Maria tapped her pale pink manicured fingernails against her water glass before she could stop herself. If she'd learned one thing growing up with her mother, and even more from visiting after she'd moved out, it was that such an obvious sign of nervousness would never be overlooked.

True to form, Elena Inesceu glanced over her rimless glasses at her daughter. Not a glare for being interrupted, nor a demand for answers right this minute. Maria knew the look from four decades of experience.

Her mother was saying yes, I see you're nervous about something. I'm going to give you time to think about it. As soon as the party's over and we get back home, though, you will tell me. Don't worry. I'll remember.

Maria smiled at her mother, more reassured by that easy read than she'd been as a teenager, and excused herself from the table. She'd been taking long drinks of mineral water as everyone else shared many toasts with pălincă, the brandy she remembered drinking from a very young age in Romania and frequently in the US.

Even a decade into hard-won sobriety, she still knew exactly how it would burn in her nose and on her tongue. How its heat would spread throughout her body before making it to her belly. The only thing she missed more was gin and tonic. Drinking enough water to need the restroom frequently was as good a distraction as any.

By the time she came back out, the three-tiered multi-colored cake was indeed front and center, but hardly anyone had touched it. Maria took half a puff pastry filled with apples and walnuts and sat down to wait out the party.

Even the cake was missing a respectable portion over two hours later when Maria took her accustomed role as designated driver in her parents' minivan full of giggling mothers and children her own age. Once everyone else was dropped off and they were nearly back to the expressway headed to Brooklyn, she decided to ask her difficult questions before her own mother had a chance to bring it up. And before they got back to her childhood home, where Elena had Maria's father to distract both of them.

"Mama, I need to ask you about some things."

Maria stopped to take a deep breath when she saw red lights in front of them. Traffic was backed up getting onto the bigger road and beyond, so she might have a lot more time than she wanted.

"You're nervous over something," her mother said. "What's wrong?" She turned her body to face Maria. Too late to put it off now.

"Nothing's wrong, don't worry," Maria said. "I have a doctor's appointment when I get back to Los Angeles, and she needs to know some of our family history."

"What business is that of a doctor? What kind of doctor?"

Maria glanced at her mother, surprised at the sharp tone in her voice. The older woman's pale, round cheeks were flushed, her forehead drawn down in what Leo called thunderbrow.

"It's nothing bad, nothing to be upset about. It's just...Leo and I have been trying..." Maria shook her head, wondering at how hard she had to work to get the words out. She must be the only daughter on the planet who had trouble saying she wanted to turn her mother into a grandmother. "We're trying to have a baby. I knew it would be hard, but even with help from a fertility doctor, it's not working. We need to know what to try next."

When the tall delivery truck ahead of them stopped long enough to shift into park, the backup lights flashing briefly before the brake lights went dim, Maria looked at her mother again. Elena stared at her for several seconds, lips pursed, then turned to look out the opposite window. The heat needle on the van was already edging up toward the red, but the shimmering waves of exhaust kept Maria from turning the air off and rolling down the windows.

When the silence stretched on long enough to feel like a solid thing, Maria turned away and rolled her eyes. She hoped she didn't have a thunderbrow of her own. Neither of her parents had ever talked about sex or health problems in their family, leaving her to learn on her own.

She'd guessed it was being shy or conservative Eastern Orthodox believers, and she'd gladly taken advantage of every educational opportunity she got in school and in a big American city. Right now her mother was acting more angry than hesitant.

"Fertility doctor," her mother said in a low voice. "Why didn't you talk to me about this before?"

"Talk to you about it?" Maria said. "You haven't been the most open about things like this. I'm not asking you to explain where babies come from. I just need to know if anyone else in the family has had trouble getting pregnant. What we're trying isn't working, even going around my problems. The doctor needs to know if something else might be wrong."

"Such things are private, Maria. Between a husband and wife. I never knew you wanted children."

"They're private, sure," Maria said. She gripped the wheel to keep from gritting her teeth. "I just need your help. I know you don't like to talk about stuff like that. I learned what I do know on my own. That's why you didn't know we wanted kids. We need your help, Mama."

"Your cousins, the ones on my side," her mother said. "They adopted babies. So many babies need families, all over the world. You and Leo, you could give such a good home."

"Well, sure, maybe we'll do that someday. But all I want is to find out why I'm not getting pregnant even with help. Maybe I want to have a baby of my own."

"You don't even have to tell anyone, Maria. Now you can find parents who look like you, and no one will ever know."

Maria stared into Elena's blue eyes, her head as overheated as the van, edging into the red. Her mother's voice wasn't so much angry now as it was desperate. Pleading.

"Is there some reason you don't want us to have a baby?" she said, dismayed at how shaky her own voice was.

"I had no warning, you never mentioned it before. Not even when you were a girl. Not after you knew about that awful infection you had and the surgery. You never even wanted to play with dolls. I thought that meant—"

"Why does it matter whether I played with dolls or not, Mama?" Maria said. "What the hell are you trying to say to me?"

"Just don't go to that doctor, please," her mother whispered, more tears spilling over, cutting through the fresh powder on her cheeks. "Some things are better left alone."

Chapter 5

MARIA JUMPED and nearly screamed when a horn sounded from behind her. The truck had moved several car lengths ahead and merged onto the slow moving expressway. When she tried to put the van into gear, her hands shook so badly she had to try twice.

"What are you saying to me, Mama? I'm not playing; this isn't something to joke about. You're scaring me half to death."

"You should be scared," her mother said, switching to Romanian. She hadn't done that for years, and it only drove the trembling deeper into Maria's gut. "I'd hoped to never go through this with you."

"Well, you are. Right now, no more games. I have an appointment with a genetic specialist the day after I get back to LA, and I damned well intend to keep it."

"My sweet Maria, no," her mother said, crossing herself repeatedly. "No, don't do this."

"Stop that! It never helps anything. Just tell me whatever it is!"

"You can't have babies," she said, her voice fast and airy. "Not just because of the scars. Not you or any of your cousins."

Maria was shaking so badly she was afraid of her foot slipping off the brake right onto the gas, sending them crashing into the high bumper of the delivery truck. All the lanes were jammed, and a row of concrete construction barricades stretching further than she could see took away even the breakdown lane.

She didn't want to hear this, she had to hear this, and she couldn't get away no matter what it turned out to be.

"What makes you think that?" Maria said. "Why would you say such a thing? It's not funny."

"I could never be more serious," she said. "May God help me, there's nothing more serious than this."

The traffic inched forward, and Maria wished the minivan would just overheat and get it over with. If steam boiled out from under the hood, she'd have an excuse to get out and walk away. Let someone else deal with all this mess.

"Okay then," she said. "You're serious. Explain it to me. Why can't any of us have babies?"

"There were such terrible things then," her mother said. She stared at the stopped traffic. "Such terrible times, under Communism. We all had to do things we didn't want to. And sometimes we didn't even know what we were doing. So many lies."

Maria waited, pushing her whole leg against the brake pedal, knuckles showing white where she gripped the wheel. Her memories of life in Romania were faint, almost like a dream she'd had before she started first grade in the US. No matter how soft and idyllic the dream, she knew it hadn't been an easy time.

"They forced many of us to have more children than we could afford to care for. I could only have one, no matter how much we tried, and we suffered for that. And people who managed to have several had even less food or medicine. We never had enough. No one did." Her mother glanced at her, then looked back out the window and took a shuddering breath. "We had a terrible outbreak of mumps in our village when you were very small. The doctors, the Communist doctors, they sent medicine that was supposed to keep the little ones healthy. Things that were supposed to make you strong, make sure you grew up and didn't catch that awful sickness."

"I am strong, Mama," Maria said, touching her mother's shoulder. "I don't understand."

"That medicine was bad," her mother said, crying again. "What they sent to the villages in the mountains, the poorest places, was poison. None of you got sick, not that we could see. But the older girls and boys, the ones who had children not long after..." She stopped, breathing deeply for several seconds. Maria squeezed her shoulder.

"Those babies had terrible problems. They had...parts in the wrong places. Missing things. Broken bodies. The lucky ones, they died before they could suffer. The awful orphanages in the cities took the ones who lived too long."

"I never heard about that before," Maria said, swallowing to keep the too-rich meal from rising into her throat. "So many things came out after the Wall fell, after Ceaușescu. How could something like that stay a secret?"

"Because we had to make a horrible choice for all of you," her mother said, grasping Maria's hand in both of hers. "We couldn't do anything with a doctor, the ones who caused all that trouble. They refused to do anything to stop it or help us. All of us were supposed to keep getting pregnant no matter how sick the babies were. Over and over again. We had to turn to something older, something more true that we could trust."

Both women jolted forward when Maria realized she was about to slowly collide with a small blue car that darted between the van and the delivery truck. Her mother let go of her hand and the seatbelt dug into Maria's neck, giving her a painful anchor back into a world that was feeling increasingly surreal. When her mother looked back into her eyes, Maria was dismayed to see that the older woman believed the insane things she was saying.

"Magic?" she said. "Even the church had to go underground then. What kind of magic?"

"We were so far away from the cities, so far away from even a twisted modern time. Magic older than the church, older than the priests, managed to survive. Such things were hard to find then like they are now, but we had nowhere else to turn. The Communist doctors, they didn't care what was happening to us, to those poor babies. We had to do something to keep from passing those terrible deformities on."

Maria's body alternated between boiling heat and freezing cold, her mind struggling to process her mother's words. If it was nothing more than some kind of crazy old spell, her doctor in Los Angeles, back in the reality she knew and understood, would find the mysteries in her DNA and Leo's and help them merge together at last.

But some part of her, steeped in those ancient mountains and stories and legends of her birth, knew it was something more.

"What did you do, Mama?"

"We all went together, all the mothers from the village, and we took our children with us. All the ones who'd had that awful medicine, from teenagers down to babies only a few months old. And we went up into the mountains where nothing could kill the old powers. A woman blessed the girls, and a man blessed the boys. That's why none of you, none of the children who'd had that poisonous medicine, had any children of your own."

"Blessed us?" Maria said, her voice a harsh gasp. "You call that blessing us, even if it was true? You can't believe that nonsense. It's the scars, the damage from the infection. That's all."

Maria's muscles were painful and frozen, no longer trembling in response to her mother's upset. Her heart pounded in her ears, but all of her insides felt like solid ice. She knew. Asking wouldn't make any difference now, but she had to anyway.

"I never had appendicitis, did I?" she said, her voice much too high in her own ears. "No infection. You got some butcher to sterilize me before I was six years old."

"My sweet Maria, you can't believe such a thing of me!"

Elena was nearly shouting, but Maria knew it was the truth. She put the van in park and turned off the engine. The tiny car in front of her barely moved five inches before the ones behind started honking.

"Please don't do that," her mother said, looking behind them with her eyes wide. "We'll talk when we get home."

She reached for the keys, but Maria yanked them out and held them in her left hand.

"Tell me the truth, Mama. Tell me what you did."

Cars on both sides started honking as people behind the van tried to edge out into those lanes. A couple of cars cut in front of them, and the horns behind only got louder.

"Someone will shoot us!" Elena cried, fumbling for the door locks. More space opened up in front of them.

"Just tell me the truth then. Thirty years of lies is more than enough. Did you get me sterilized?"

Motion in the rear view mirror caught Maria's eye as someone stepped out of a huge gray SUV and walked toward them. Her mother turned to stare at the man, her eyes wide and her face pale. She finally sat forward with her face in her hands, shaking her head.

"Yes! You were sick with pain in your belly, but I don't know what it was. I went to the same doctor who helped me, the same way. We could not feed so many in our village, so he helped me after you were born. And with that poison...all those poor babies...we had to!"

Maria's hand was no longer trembling, but her numb fingers had a difficult time finding a grip on the key. She was more tempted than she cared to admit to leave it in park, walk away from her mother's harsh sobs. Deal with whatever happened rather than what her mother had just told her. She started the car and jerked the gearshift into drive instead.

Neither woman spoke as the traffic finally broke up or on the painfully long drive. Not until Maria put the van in park again and dropped the keys into her mother's hand.

"I don't have anything else to say to you," Maria said, wiping traitorous tears from her cheeks. "I hope it was worth it."

"You won't go to that doctor, will you? Please, if you promise me that, I'll know it was all worth it."

"That's none of your damned business. Whether I manage to get pregnant or not, you'll never know about it. My children will never even know your name."

Chapter 6

Eight years ago

THE OPEN-AIR CAFE sat high on the cliff over the Pacific Ocean, with nothing in sight but deep blue water and landscaping carefully designed to look natural. The best-looking valets Maria had ever seen made expensive cars disappear, along with any thoughts of worrying about the cost in such an exclusive setting. The noise and madness of LA seemed years away rather than barely two hours.

The tasteful white awnings, tile, and tablecloths showcased the sparkling waves more effectively than any art museum could have. Food and drink as good as anything further south in the city brought Maria here with friends or visiting family members. She led her more paranoid clients to believe this was the most private location outside of one of the national parks. She was delighted to take any opportunity she could to escape to fundamental peace and quiet.

Maria sipped her raspberry tea, breathing in the scent of her childhood friend's coffee. That would have suited her so much better, but she was trying to be good. Ana's blue eyes were bloodshot and dark smudges gave away how tired she still was. She'd barely started the eight-hour adjustment to New York time when she added three more hours onto the burden by flying to California. A leisurely brunch by the sea was the best jetlag cure either of them could imagine.

"Is the coffee helping?" Maria said.

"Not yet." Ana hid a yawn behind her hand before taking another long drink. "Tastes good, though. When did you start drinking tea? Some kind of California thing?"

"Hardly," Maria said. "Neither of us would have lasted long out here if it had been. The house came with a built-in espresso machine."

"Then you should stop trying to inhale my coffee and get your own," Ana said, smiling.

Maria smiled back. She hadn't planned on telling Ana about seeing a new fertility specialist, but she was getting tired of keeping the secret.

"My doctor said it's a good idea to switch," she said. "Just to be safe."

"Safe?" Ana rubbed her eyes and blinked at Maria. "What, are you trying to get pregnant or something?"

"Well, yeah, we have been for a while now. Didn't my mother mention it? She's not exactly on board with the whole idea."

"No, she wouldn't be," Ana said. "She didn't mention a word. Too busy quizzing me about everything else in your life to get around to that. When did you last talk to her, Mar?"

Maria shook her head and looked out at the ocean. The Pacific was calm from so high up, the early sunlight tracing level, regular waves. She wished she felt the same. With Leo or even with her girlhood friend, she was terribly on edge lately from all the new hormones.

She frowned. "I don't know, around the time we started going to fertility doctors. Two years, I guess."

"That's too long not to talk to your mother," Ana said, her full lips curving down. "She's worried sick about both of you."

"She never bothers to call me, Ana. Not anymore. Listen, what did you mean, she wouldn't be on board with us trying?"

Ana groaned and closed her eyes.

"I did say that, didn't I? I should keep my mouth shut until I get over this wretched jet lag."

"Too late now," Maria said. "Out with it."

"It's not for me to tell, is it? Things between you and your mother? I don't want to be that person in the middle."

"Look at it this way, my Ana," Maria said, watching the waiter approach with perfect timing for refills. "My mother put us both in the middle, not me. It wasn't enough to get me sterilized before I even started to grow up. Not for my mother. She had to hire some witch doctor to keep me from having mutated babies when I was still a baby myself."

"A what?" Ana said. "You're not making any sense."

"A witch doctor. Some kind of folk nonsense back in Transylvania. Last time we talked, Mama told me she got some old crone to bless me so I wouldn't have deformed children. Mama believed a story about bad Communist medicine thirty years ago that made mutated babies. Leo and I are paying for that bullshit now. Well, our insurance is paying for every medical test under the sun to prove not a word of it was true."

"I don't know about any kind of bad medicine," Ana said, stirring organic honey into her fresh coffee. "And this whole idea isn't thirty years old, either. That's really what she told you?"

Cold settled into Maria's belly despite the boiling hot tea. She'd done her best to put her mother's delusions behind her when all the tests for abnormalities came back clear, but now her best friend was threatening to drag her right back into them.

"What else would she have told me?" she said. "She let some butcher cut me up, made a mess of my belly."

"You said you've been trying to get pregnant for how long?" Ana said. "Three years?"

"Four years. Two since we started seeing specialists. Please don't tell me she made all of that up for some sick reason, Ana."

The other woman sighed, rubbing at her mouth.

"I'm the wrong person to be telling you this," Ana said. "Maybe you will go back to New York with me before I return to Romania. Talk to your mother."

"No, not about this!" Maria tried to ignore everyone staring at them. "My mother's lies cost us years when I was younger, when we should have been trying. I can't ever trust her again. You have to tell me, please. Maybe it's something my new doctor can help with."

"Not this, Maria. Not a medical doctor, anyway. This is a lot older than that. Have you ever heard the word *strigoi*?"

"Not that I...I don't think so."

Maria was careful to look into Ana's blue eyes instead of into her teacup, but she was lying. A spark of recognition, slow and faint at first but gaining speed, moved out from her brain into her jittery nerve endings.

Ana shrugged. "Not many people our age have, I suppose. I had a bad habit of hiding and listening in whenever I could. Once people travel more, and definitely with the internet, such things die out or become jokes. It wasn't a joke to our parents, or theirs. Some of the older ones said *Vida* instead, but the legends were the same. With either one, they spoke of the undead."

"Surely you don't mean zombies?" Maria said, wishing she could laugh.

"Not really, not like you know today. They came back, but not to eat up brains and wander around. These returned to their families, almost like they never died. They were said to live on energy. Or on blood."

"Now you're telling me my mother believes in vampires? She hated that Dracula nonsense as much as everyone else back there."

"Like the zombies, this is not really the same," Ana said. "No capes or bats or long pointy teeth. Only an uneasy soul that won't stay in the ground the way it should."

"Okay then." Maria took a long, deep breath, trying to slow her heart. "Say my mother believes in this craziness. What the hell does it have to do with me, Ana? Why would she want to keep me from having children?"

"That's because if a strigoi lasts long enough, it can return in a body. And it can even have children who are the same. Some families believe that happened to them years ago, so they bury each other in certain ways to make sure no one comes back. You know those customs, with the whiskey and the garlic and watching the body. Those who don't follow the old ways..."

Ana paused, eyebrows raised.

"Are doomed!" Maria said more loudly than she meant to.

Both women fell into a fit of giggling. Ana sounded like nothing more than the giddy high school girl, overjoyed with seeing Maria again after years of nothing but letters between them. They'd invented this silly game when Ana tried to explain the last tumultuous years of Communism to Maria.

More appropriate patrons glancing at them only made the laughter worse. Trying to keep quiet made her head pound, but Maria welcomed the distraction from the hot tingling in her hands and feet.

"So it is said." Ana wiped away tears, her color almost normal instead of pale exhaustion. "You must remember our parents grew up so isolated from the world in those mountains, and Communism only made that worse. They abandoned the last of the oldest villages just this year, no one more than a cleanup committee to keep the grand-mothers happy ever go there anymore. Just as well with such bad memories. All they had to hold on to was some ancient magic when life was so terrible."

"I don't see how that justifies what she thought she did to me," Maria said. "Much less what she really did. I saw the scans. Whoever did this ripped up my insides."

Ana grimaced. "I'm not saying anything justifies what happened then in more than just Romania, except people were trying to survive when that was almost impossible. I know your Mama loves you, and she's worried about you."

This time Maria stared out at the water instead of looking at her friend. The bright sunlight provided an acceptable excuse for her watering eyes.

"I know, Ana. Maybe when this is all over, I'll see her again."

Ana probably didn't realize it, not with her slow-moving jetlagged brain, but she'd just given Maria the target her increasingly frantic mind needed.

Strigoi.

Whatever that word meant, wherever it came from, she intended to remember anything that affected her so strongly. To learn every-thing she possibly could about it.

From addiction to law school to the most unsympathetic jury, she'd never found a problem she couldn't master once she learned enough. Some foolish ancient Transylvanian folklore would not defeat her.

Chapter 7

Seven years ago

Leo sat beside Maria in the crowded waiting room, his elbow jammed painfully against the metal arm of the chair. His fingers were going numb from the pressure of his wife's grip, but he didn't dare let go.

Several overstuffed loveseats and sofas were arranged throughout the space, all covered in some variation of pink or blue fabric, but the two of them never sat in those. Neither mentioned believing the more comfortable chairs should be reserved for the couples already winning the procreation race. They just headed to the uncomfortable overflow area every time.

The nice furniture was usually full of fertility on display, and today was no exception. Men and women took the loveseats, invariably with his arm around her, mixed comfortably with several pairs of women in variations of the same pose. The sofas held couples of every gender variety with a predictable third party, a younger woman clearly in an outsider position. She sat on the other side of the couple, beside the woman if there was one, rarely in the middle. Despite that distance, the bond between the three was clear.

That last possible arrangement was what brought Leo here with

Maria after years of repeatedly trying every other option available to produce a baby of their own. They'd both checked out perfectly healthy several times, aside from her scarred abdomen, yet nothing worked.

He'd been immensely relieved when she finally agreed to stop the IVF after enduring month after month of anxiety and hope followed by heartbreak and depression so bottomless it frightened him. The drugs for the egg harvest and the potential side effects frightened him even more. At least the doctors here agreed they already had more than enough healthy eggs. No one could explain why Maria's healthy uterus kept rejecting them.

Three perky nurses with bouncy ponytails and bright pastel uniforms decorated with balloons, pacifiers, and bottles stepped out one after the other, calling people back. Sometimes Mr. and Mrs., sometimes two of each, names hyphenated or not. The nurses were very careful to call all of the names every time, including the surrogates. Leo wondered when—or if—they and their as yet undiscovered surrogate would move over to the sofas.

Maria squeezed his hand, or he thought she did, before she clasped both of hers in her lap. Leo sighed at the simple pleasure of moving his arm up and around his wife. He moved his fingers as little as he could, hoping she wouldn't notice him trying to cope with the painful pins and needles.

The excellent insurance they had through the studio had been wonderful. At first. Leo knew many of the couples they'd encountered in waiting rooms over the past decade had been paying everything out of their own pockets. Most of them likely didn't have the financial resources of a Hollywood talent agent and his movie and TV intellectual property attorney wife.

Leo was sympathetic and wondered how they managed, but that didn't stop his mental tally of what he and Maria had spent already. They were well into the hundreds of thousands of dollars for this so far fruitless effort. He feared surrogacy would put them perilously close to seven figures.

The last threesome who'd been waiting when they arrived, two men and a heavily pregnant woman, got up and walked back with the redheaded nurse. A slow churn that worsened with each visit started up in Leo's belly.

He'd gotten through the first eye-popping rounds of copayments and later full payments by reminding himself how hard they both worked. What was the money for, if they couldn't do something his bride wanted so badly? When they passed double, then triple the cost of an adoption, he'd mentioned it as gently as he could. *Not yet*, she'd said, tears standing in her lovely green eyes.

As the cost mounted and Leo struggled to keep it out of his mind for more than a couple of hours at a time, he knew *not yet* wasn't going to hold up much longer. He didn't want to be that person, that husband, but he couldn't keep watching so much money disappear. Especially when she'd never really told him why it was so damned important to her.

"Mr. and Mrs. Sabov?"

Leo stood, smiled, and held out his hand.

Chapter 8

Six years ago

THE CAR WAS a little piece of heaven to Maria from the instant she saw it on the dealer's showroom floor. A pearlescent white Mercedes, pale blue leather interior. Loaded with every possible amenity to show off what could be done, even if hardly anyone would ever pay for such extravagance. Five years and many hours and miles hadn't dulled the gleam or the luxury for her. As Maria fell deeper into the pit in her empty belly, and further into desperation, her car still brought her comfort. Her car made her feel safe.

The big sedan purred quietly, the fan switching on and off to compensate for the air conditioner. Chopin filled the space and her ears, but Maria's body refused to respond to her beloved soothing music. She gripped the wheel tight enough to make her wrists ache and stared at the small brick ranch house across the street.

The neighborhood was neat and modest, with clean sidewalks and well-maintained lawns in front of the tidy houses. This was much more like where she'd grown up in New York and Leo had in Cleveland than the domain of professional gardeners and landscapers where they lived now.

Those modest origins explained a little of why he'd been so thrilled to buy her the Mercedes, back when they were really getting established in LA. Before either of them could have imagined the mess Maria's head had become. He hadn't shed an ounce of his Midwestern practicality, taking her out during the clearance sales for new models. But that light in his eyes, the confidence in his smile and his step when he walked back out with the key, reminded her why she'd fallen in love with him in the first place.

Leo didn't simply talk a good game, making her and everyone else a bunch of promises he couldn't keep. He worked his ass off until he made all of it come true and more, especially for Maria. That determination and previous success, for her and his clients, made it so much harder on him now that he and everyone else were running out of suggestions for why they still failed to conceive.

Maria checked her hair and makeup, though she wasn't sure why. None of the practitioners, whether of Reiki, witchcraft, or gemstones, gave a damn what she looked like. After over a dozen failed attempts, with more than half proclaiming her healed, Maria sometimes wondered if they only cared whether her credit card was valid.

"That's not fair, Counselor," she said to her reflection, then got out of the car.

This woman came highly recommended after a focused online and in-person search, and Maria hoped she would be as dedicated and sincere as all the others had been. Whatever their method—crystals, cards, or chanting—all the healers either believed in what they were doing, or they were missing their calling as breathtaking actors and actresses.

And still all of the medical procedures and three attempts at surrogacy had failed.

Once she got herself moving, Maria strode up the sidewalk toward the basement entry as if heading into a courtroom. She'd learned long ago to exude confidence when she was terrified inside. In her own way, she was as good at acting as anyone she represented.

Maria never walked into a courtroom or negotiation unprepared, and she'd never dug more deeply into any problem in her life. Short of getting on a plane right now and going to Transylvania herself to investigate, she'd learned everything she possibly could about her mother's crazy beliefs and crazier actions. Logic and determination crashed headlong into fear and superstition. If doctors and Western medicine were going to keep failing her, Maria was ready to follow Ana's lead and turn to something older.

A middle-aged woman several inches shorter than Maria answered the door. She was wearing a full typical tourist Gypsy outfit, complete with swirling red skirts and noisy jewelry. Her dark green eyes and olive skin at least seemed correct. Before she could say a word, Maria spoke in Romanian. She was in no mood for shows and games.

"I'm Maria. I was born in Transylvania, but I grew up in the US. I need your help if you're willing to give it."

The woman tilted her head and looked Maria up and down, no doubt evaluating everything from her simple gold jewelry to her Jimmy Choo heels. Maria wasn't in full lawyer mode today, trading her black suits for gray linen pants and a jacket. She wasn't in attack mode either, but she insisted on being taken seriously.

"Come on in, Maria," she said, her English perfect. "I'm Julia. I grew up here too. Studied under my Romanii grandmother. Happy to drop the act so we can talk."

Maria followed Julia into a basement sitting room decorated like what most people assumed a Gypsy caravan must look like on the inside. Multicolored fabrics covered the walls and ceiling, and thick cushions sat in front of a small table. The expected crystal ball was on the table, and candles glowed from every other surface.

"Just ignore all this," Julia said, waving a hand toward the room as she opened a door to the right. "No matter how many times I explain what I really do, most people expect the stereotypical getup. Coffee or tea?"

"Tea would be wonderful, thank you."

The kitchen at the top of the stairs was bright and cheerful with yellow walls and curtains, a sharp contrast from the mysterious space in the basement. Maria recognized plates and bowls from Romania displayed on shelves, their delicate raised designs not for everyday use. Julia brought out sturdy white porcelain mugs and saucers.

"I appreciate the break from the smoke and mirrors." Julia put a heavy black kettle on the stove and sat across from Maria. "What can I do for you?"

"I hope you can help me figure out why I'm not getting pregnant," Maria said, wrapping her fingers around the cool mug. "We've tried every medical option, even surrogacy."

"Why me, though? I can give you a blessing, but that's not my normal thing."

"I know." Maria took her usual deep breath before she crossed her last rational line. "I'm here because I heard you can remove curses. Is that right?"

Julia scowled. "A curse to keep you from getting pregnant that would keep a surrogate from getting pregnant too? I don't mean to sound rude, but what gave you that idea?"

Maria couldn't breathe for a moment, looking into those no-nonsense green eyes. The typical song and dance might have made this easier after all.

She'd said it easily enough to all the others, maybe because she didn't expect them to believe her. She had a strong feeling Julia would. When the kettle started to sing and Julia got up, Maria found her own voice.

Chapter 9

"MY MOTHER THOUGHT ALL the kids were given bad medicine by Communist doctors," Maria said. "She and my aunts and uncles thought we'd have deformed babies. She got a shitty doctor to sterilize me, then got some old woman to bless me so I couldn't have any children."

"She called that a blessing, huh?" Julia said, pouring tea for both of them. "Any chance the medicine part was true?"

"I don't know." Maria rubbed her jaws and the constant ache there. "My husband and I both had genetic screenings, and nothing seems to be wrong with my eggs or any other part of me besides my fallopian tubes. The eggs just don't work. I mean, doctors can put them together with my husband's sperm, but it doesn't take no matter what we try."

Julia held the tea up to her nose, breathing deeply.

"I'm guessing you've tried other people like me, too."

"I've tried everything," Maria said, rolling her eyes. "New Age woo to old time voodoo, and everything in between. Several people have declared me cured once I paid the bill, but here I am. You're the first person I've found from Romania. And the first to drop the act instead of trying to dazzle me."

"Hazards of a town full of actors, I suppose," Julia said. "Listen, I've never run into anything like this. How does your husband feel?"

Maria stared into the dark brown tea. She tilted the sugar spoon, watching the sparkling white stream falling into the cup.

"He's gone along with everything medically," she said quietly. "I think he's getting upset about the cost. He doesn't know about this part. Not with you or any of the others."

Julia stared into Maria's eyes again, her head tilted to one side.

"Okay," she said with a nod. "As soon as we're finished here, I'll tune in and see what I can do."

Before Maria was ready, she was following Julia back down to the extravagant basement room.

"I'm sure this all seems a bit much to you," Julia said, shrugging. "I've gotten into the habit of working down here. Do you mind the cushions on the floor?"

Maria shook her head, then slipped off her shoes and sat on a thick blue cushion on one side of the small fabric-covered table. Julia sat on a red one opposite her.

"What are you going to do?" she said. "I've had a couple of unpleasant surprises."

Julia smiled. "You're not insisting on flash and glamour, so I won't do any of that. I'll see how you feel. See if anything's hanging around you that shouldn't be. My grandmother did use the crystal ball, but I'm comfortable without it if you are."

She held out her hands, and Maria covered them with her own. Julia's many rings were sharp and cold.

"Just relax," Julia said. "Take a few deep breaths. Close your eyes."

Maria breathed as deeply as she could with her heart beating so fast and hard. She was certain Julia would hear it or feel it in her hands. After a few seconds of listening to the other woman's slow breathing, she opened her eyes.

Julia was still as a statue, her plump, dark red lips slightly parted. On her next deep exhalation, she pulled her left hand free and held it palm down over Maria's head.

"Everything seems fine so far," Julia said in a whispery voice. "Doing okay?"

"I'm fine."

Julia moved her hand down, never touching Maria, tracing an outline of her shape. When her palm was barely an inch from Maria's stubbornly flat abdomen, she stopped.

"There is something here," she said, her mouth turning down. "I can't tell what, but it's been here for a while. Not all that deep. Very strong."

"What are you going to do?" Maria whispered. She forced her hand to relax its grip on Julia's.

"Feels like I could shift it enough to move it out. Never felt something like this. All through your belly, but it radiates out." She moved her hand back until it was over a foot away. "I think it pushes even further." She shook her head, her brow furrowed. "Underneath that, though. So deep. So old. I can't quite remember..."

Julia's words drifted off, and she was still. Her fingers slowly curled around her palm, the rings flashing in the candlelight. Julia drew her whole body back, as if she'd touched a red-hot cooktop. Her face went pale before she opened her eyes.

"What?" Maria said, trying to hold on when Julia pulled her other hand away. "What is it?"

"I can't," Julia said, staring at the crystal ball. "I can't do anything. I'm sorry, Maria."

"No, you said you could move it," Maria said. "At least tell me what it is!"

"It's like your mother said, and very effective. You won't be able to have children. Older magic than I've ever felt before."

"But why?" Maria reached toward Julia but she drew away, getting to her feet and stepping toward the door. "Why won't you help me?"

"I like you, Maria. I'm sure you'd make a wonderful mother. But it's not to be. Some curses were never meant to be passed along. Live your life with your husband. Let this pass away from your mind. I'm sorry."

Maria stood, watching Julia move farther away from her.

"How can you tell me I have some kind of curse but you won't help me get rid of it?"

"The deeper curse is something no one can remove," Julia said. "It is part of you. Someone may be able to remove the magic, the spell that prevents you from having children. I hope anyone who could will understand why they should not."

"Wait!" Maria cried. "If I say it, what I've heard, will you at least tell me if I'm right? Isn't it the least you can do?"

"Please don't put me in that—"

Maria whispered the word Ana used, the word so strange and too familiar.

"*Strigoi.*"

Julia flinched. Maria was sure her twitching hands wanted to cross herself, over and over again like she'd seen her mother and old women in Romania do. At least Julia had confirmed what Maria needed to focus on next.

"I'll be sure to pass that much along if I ever find someone else," Maria said, stepping into her shoes. "If I even bother to try. What do I owe you, Julia?"

"Nothing." She folded her hands and looked at the ground, the tiny brass bells around her neck tinkling. "I truly am sorry. Please go. And please do not return."

Chapter 10

Five years ago

No MATTER what else was going on in her life, snow always made Maria giddy as a schoolgirl. The luxurious log cabin perched near the top of a mountain pass in North Carolina, surrounded by dark pine trees mixed with pale, bare hardwood branches. Thick, heavy flakes poured down fast enough to sound like feathery rain.

The soaring wood and stone living room was warm and bright, but she stayed out on the deck as long as she could stand it. The snow transformed early afternoon into late evening like magic.

Maria finally stepped inside, heat from the roaring fire melting the snow in her hair in a few seconds. The two-story windows let her see the storm just fine, but she'd head back out to feel the cold against her skin before bedtime. Paul and Gary assured her getting back down off the mountain in a couple of days wouldn't be a problem. They were less than twenty miles outside of Asheville, and the forecast called for warmer temperatures. She hoped they were snowed in for at least a few days herself.

Maria shook her coat and scarf before hanging them on the coat tree carved to look like a real tree by the sliding glass doors. She wore the same winter vacation gear of worn flannel shirt and blue jeans as her host. Such casual clothing, old and comfortable rather than aged by a stylist, was one of many of Maria's beloved sins that would horrify most of her Hollywood clients.

"Get over here and have some hot chocolate," Paul said. "I'm getting cold just watching you out there."

"This is what I miss most living in LA," she said. "A break from sunny and bloody seventy-five degrees."

"Just about everyone in these mountains would kill for that sometime in mid-January."

Paul Mullins was one of her first clients, a novelist from back East trying to navigate the tricky ways of Hollywood, and a new pen name, without getting eaten alive. That initial publishing and movie success had turned into a long-standing friendship between the four of them. Paul and Gary provided the vital antidote for East Coast people living on the West Coast for so long.

Maria sat beside Paul on an overstuffed tan sofa close to the fire. She could smell the booze in his oversized coffee mug, but she knew hers would be safe. They'd been friends far too long for him to make a mistake like that.

"Send them my way for the warm weather," she said. "As long as I get to see one good snowstorm every year."

The massive ottoman was big enough for both their legs and an enticing stack of folders and notebooks. Maria didn't want to push, especially when she hadn't seen Paul in almost a year. But she was more anxious by the second to dig into what he'd dug up for her. He smiled and shook his head, his curly shoulder-length silver hair glinting in the firelight.

"I should make you sit here and talk writer gossip with me for at least an hour before I let you see any of that."

"I'll gossip," she said, trying not to laugh. "You know I will. I was just thinking of Gary. You'll have to repeat everything when he gets home, and you don't tell it nearly as well as I do."

"You're getting this flattery thing backwards, young lady," Paul said. "I told you that West Coast lifestyle would rot your brain."

He leaned forward and picked up the stack, flipping through one of the folders too fast for her to see.

"You're pure evil, Paul."

"Mission accomplished." He grinned and dropped the pile in her lap. "Quite an interesting bunch of tales you sent me wandering into. Gonna tell me what this is all about?"

"Maybe I plan to write a book," Maria said.

She scanned through the printed documents, focusing on the highlighted areas and Paul's neat handwritten notes. She wasn't about to admit how badly her mother's lies and Ana's tales of the undead had gotten under her skin.

Sensible Julia being so frightened had pushed Maria so far over the edge that she could never turn back to rational pursuits.

"Maybe you should write that book." Paul's somber tone got her full attention. "This gets a bit slimy, hon. Maybe more than even a badass Hollywood lawyer wants to deal with."

"Slimy how?"

"Taking advantage of an old woman with dementia, for starters," he said before finishing his adult hot chocolate. "She's the best source for what you're looking for. At least the only one who'll talk to you."

"I'm sorry," Maria said. "I didn't meant to drag you into something like this."

"No, don't apologize," he said, shrugging. "I didn't talk to her myself. My extensive network of spies did the dirty work. I got a hell of a book idea out of the whole thing, too. I'm just saying you want to think this over before you go haring off to Austria. And maybe ask that gorgeous man of yours to handle the casting when they make the movie of the book I'm fixing to write."

"I'll see what I can arrange," Maria said, opening another folder. "This her?"

A stern middle-aged woman stared out of a black and white photo, dark hair in a strict bun on top of her head. Her severe military uniform and accusing expression reminded Maria of Igor, the old party boss in her mother's village.

"That's her back in the eighties," Paul said. "Poor thing. We all had bad hair back then."

"Even you?"

"Especially me! Trying to fit into the litt-tra-chure crowd, writing butch espionage novels, forcing myself to act straight all the way up to my poor hair. There's a reason my author photos were all from a safe distance."

"What's this place in Austria?" Maria said, frowning. Folklore from the wrong part of the world wasn't going to help her. "Magda Schmidt? She's not from Romania?"

"Magda Lupescu, originally from Transylvania just like you. Married a good Austrian not long after the Soviet Union self-destructed, then moved back home with him. Second marriage for both. Best for both to get the hell out of Romania. Magda was known as a bit of an enforcer, not at all beloved. When Mr. Schmidt passed away a couple of years ago, all their children from various marriages got together and gave Mrs. Schmidt a one-way ticket to retirement. Nice place, really. We should all be so lucky."

"If she was that high up, why would she talk to me?" Maria said.

"Well, that's the slimy bit, hon," Paul said.

He got to his feet, holding out a hand. Maria let him pull her up and followed him into the kitchen. The view to the woods rising up behind the house was nearly as spectacular as the front, with floor to ceiling windows behind a gleaming stainless steel and granite chef's kitchen.

Paul's early success with espionage suspense novels published under John Richards transitioned beautifully into political thrillers published as James Mitchell. His long-standing Eastern European connections were promising to work out just as well for Maria.

"Magda's getting prone to mistaken identity," Paul said, filling each of their mugs with fresh hot chocolate from a pot on the cooktop. He added whiskey to his own. "Sort of funny considering her previous line of work. With only a little bit of encouragement, she'll recognize you as her sister, Dorina."

Maria shook her head as she grabbed bowls of pretzels and chips. A veritable mountain of carbs and salt. Yet another thing her West Coast friends would be horrified by.

"And when Dorina visits next time," she said, "won't she wonder why her sister thinks she just saw her?"

"Not likely." Paul threw two more logs on the fire before he rejoined Maria on the couch. "Dorina passed away not long after the Soviet Union did. These days, Magda sees her in any woman your age with dark hair. She can't keep the timeline straight in any case, no idea what decade she thinks it is. If that doesn't work, mentioning that creepy Igor back in Transylvania you told me about does the trick. He's a damned piece of work himself."

Maria stared into the flames. She'd handled a few cases of family members trying to take advantage of authors or screenwriters with memory problems. Not much terrified her more than ending up that way herself.

"Thus the slimy part," she said.

"Very much so. Listen, Maria, you sure you want to get into this? My friend over there isn't exactly the shy type, but she was shook up by this whole thing. I say you just turn the fake book into a real one and leave this one alone."

"You've told me more than once about how an idea gets under your skin," she said. "You can't give it up, even if I warn you how much you're going to have to pay me to keep you out of legal trouble." Maria looked up into his blue eyes. He nodded. "This one's got me, Paul. Too far back and way too deep for me to walk away. I appreciate you more than you know for getting me this far."

Paul grunted. "Figured you'd say that. Now listen to me. I'm the biggest skeptic on the face of the earth. I've laughed at a thousand stories of folk magic and religion. I thought the crazy occult stuff the Nazis were into was the worst. But something about Ms. Magda and her tales of decapitation and poisoning the grave has me spooked through and through. Think you'll tell me about it someday? When it's all over?"

"I'll most likely be telling you it's a bunch of nonsense like all the rest," Maria said. She never lied to Paul, and she hated to do it now. She couldn't seem to help herself. "If anything comes of my visit with her, I'll give you the scoop."

Paul stared at her for several seconds. Maria worked with enough writers to know when she was being examined and evaluated, like an x-ray machine trained on her mind. She also knew how to look right back and try to hide what she had to. Even when she probably wasn't hiding a damned thing.

"Okay then," he said. "You know I'll hold you to that, whether you mean it right now or not. My one condition is you let me set up the identification you'll need. These things are harder than they used to be, especially if you've never done it before. No way I'm letting someone else mess this up and it gets traced back to my high-powered West Coast lawyer."

"You're expecting me to remember a new name on top of all the rest?"

"Not at all, sweetheart," he said, grinning. "An old one. Don't you think it's time we brought Mr. and Mrs. Paul Mullins back from the dead?"

Maria gulped her mouthful of hot chocolate down, probably burning the back of her throat in an effort to keep from spitting it out all over Paul's gorgeous tan furniture. The most honest, true laughter she'd felt in a long while brought more tears to her eyes. She leaned against Paul's shoulder while she caught her breath.

"You're telling me we're going to pretend to be married now? When you're legally married to Gary in all fifty states?"

"That's exactly what I'm telling you, Mrs. Mullins," he said. "Easiest thing in the world for both of us to remember, and a lot easier to blend in most places as Maria Mullins than as Sabov or Inesceu. Deal?"

"I would not presume to argue with you, my dear husband," Maria said. "Maria Mullins it is."

He plucked a slim notebook out of the stack, the same vinyl-covered model Maria used herself. He handed it to her with one of her favorite blue ink pens.

"This is what you need to know going in."

Chapter 11

Five years ago

The illusion was nearly perfect.

The cobblestone street was lined with bright, lively restaurants, shops, and services like post offices, salons, and banks. A cinema at the end of the row, proclaiming itself home of the classics, advertised movies and TV shows from before Maria was born. All were available with either subtitles in multiple languages or support for advanced hearing aids.

Young, energetic, and unusually attentive men and women staffed those businesses. Pensioners and retirees from all over the world strolled up and down the immaculate sidewalks, smiling and greeting Maria where she waited on a comfortable park bench.

She had to admit the facade was every bit as good as anything Disney ever created in Southern California, Florida, or anywhere else. None of the residents would even guess the community was in Austria rather than elsewhere in Europe unless too many employees said "*Gross gott.*"

Only by looking closely would anyone notice the stylish and well-disguised medical alert necklaces or pins the residents wore. The emergency call buttons on nearly every gas lamppost were even harder to spot, as were the wide aisles in the shops made to accommodate gurneys and emergency equipment.

Maria alternated between shuffling her notes and tugging at the quaint outfit she'd borrowed from the administration of this high-end retirement facility. Depending upon the mental state and nationality of the resident, the director tactfully encouraged visitors to play along with the atmosphere.

She'd been delighted to spot the vintage black jacket and skirt, and she had to admit the fit and cut were more flattering than she expected from Soviet-era clothïng. Maria also knew why such wool fabrics had fallen out of style after twenty minutes of trying to keep everything from touching her sensitive skin. She was having an even harder time not fidgeting with one of Paul's suggestions, an asymmetrical black brooch concealing her digital recorder.

A young man Maria had spoken to earlier, now stationed behind the bar of the coffee shop across the street, waved to get her attention. The space was decorated more like a mid-century Paris bistro than a Starbucks, and it served as a meeting place for residents and visitors. An older woman walked toward the shop, accompanied by one of the staff members dressed like Maria.

The woman was several years older than Maria's mother, and she wore a dark gray skirt and jacket that had to have come from her own Soviet-era closet. Her iron gray hair was drawn into the same severe bun from Paul's photos. She walked as if she were marching before a review stand in a military parade.

Maria met the young man at a table on the sidewalk, already set with her double espresso and a steaming mug of black tea. Her hands shook when she put her notebook and pen down beside the tiny white porcelain cup. He didn't seem to notice. If Paul's sources and contacts had done their jobs correctly, neither he nor anyone else at the faux village would think she was anything more than a writer researching Cold War lifestyles and choices for women.

"Just let me know if you need anything, Mrs. Mullins," Erick said.

Every new acceptance of her identity reassured her tremendously, and the inside joke with Paul eased her nerves a tiny bit.

Erick's Romanian was perfect with only a hint of a German accent. He pulled out Maria's tastefully aged wrought iron chair along with a matching one with a bright floral cushion for the guest of honor.

"And don't be surprised if she thinks you're her sister," he said softly as Magda arrived. "Good afternoon, Mrs. Schmidt. You have company."

"I'm quite certain I know who this is, Erick," she said, glancing at his discreet name tag as he walked around to help her sit. "Thank you for the tea. Do you think I don't recognize my own sister?"

"Of course not," Erick said. He looked into Maria's eyes, and she smiled. "It's wonderful that she wants to write a book about you, isn't it? Just let me know if either of you need anything and enjoy your visit."

"Did he say you're writing a book, Dorina?" Magda said.

The older woman sipped her tea, glancing at Erick. Maria's heart sank at the confused look and need for help even though she'd gotten her sister's name. Maria's chance to learn anything from this woman may have already passed.

"I told Dorina you'd be perfect for her book," the young man said without missing a beat. "No one knows more about women's lives under Communism than you."

"Indeed I do," she said, nodding once. "We had many difficult choices to make, but in a way, we had more freedom than women do even now."

As Erick smiled and walked away, Maria's nearly constant doubts surged all around her. Maybe she should write this book after all, follow her fascination with the piles of research Paul had reluctantly supplied.

That at least would make a hell of a lot more sense than sinking deeper into this obsession that already felt far too much like addiction. Maybe her next appointment should be with a shrink instead of another fertility specialist or another relic of Romania's past.

"What did you want to ask me, Dorina?" Magda said. "Is there a problem with my grandchildren?"

Maria didn't detect anything like sisterly warmth, but she'd take any help she could get. She took a deep breath and flashed her best reassuring in the face of a difficult situation smile.

"All the children are fine, Magda. I'd like to hear more about those choices you mentioned, the ways you had more freedom before the USSR fell."

Mrs. Schmidt talked for a few minutes about greater equality in jobs and pay between men and women. Greater struggles for food and survival. The increasing drain on Romania when the massive Parliament went up in Bucharest. Her words trailed off, and she stared out into the busy street. She turned back to Maria with the same confused look she'd shown Erick.

"I'm sorry, Dorina. I can't seem to remember what you wanted to ask me? Was it about the children?"

"That's quite all right," Maria said. "All of this has been about children in one way or another. I'm curious about how women were able to make choices under Communism, maybe differently from afterwards."

After two more perfectly clear conversations followed by bewildered pauses when Mrs. Schmidt lost the thread and her place in time, Maria had just about decided to give up on this lead, no matter how promising it seemed in the beginning. She might never find another of Igor's counterparts so far away from Romania, isolated and willing to talk. But this poor woman barely seemed able to focus for more than a few minutes at a time.

She glanced down at her notes, hoping for a miracle even as she planned her graceful exit. Paul had supplied background and suggestions as detailed as Maria did for her own cases. His Eastern Europe connections had proven invaluable, but he'd gone deeper than that. The answer jumped out from the top of a section called "Interviewing Dementia Patients."

Risky as it felt, she had to get specific.

"Magda, let me ask you about something else. I do wonder about women's choices when it came to having children. And I've always been fascinated with the burial rituals in Transylvania, especially in the more remote mountain villages. Can you tell me about your work in these areas?"

Maria kept a firm grip on her best courtroom blank expression as Mrs. Schmidt's confused, pleasant demeanor vanished in an instant. She focused like a laser, face firm, eyes slightly narrowed. The strict Communist Party leader had returned, just like Paul suspected she would with the right prompt.

The game was finally on.

Chapter 12

"THAT IS a strange topic to bring up, Dorina," Magda Schmidt said, taking a deep breath and leaning back in her chair. "I wonder why you would turn to that now."

"This is one of the reasons I'm returning to Romania," Maria said, in full attorney calm mode even though her heart was pounding. "A problem is developing, you see. A problem that had never been there until now. I must be certain the sort of trouble you worked so hard to prevent doesn't gain a foothold in future generations."

Mrs. Schmidt stared at Maria for several seconds without moving. She abruptly turned toward the coffee shop, beckoning Erick over with a sharp gesture.

He smiled indulgently at Maria and started toward them, ready to humor whatever the odd request might be. Maria knew every scrap of humor had vanished. Her throat was too dry to swallow, her mind lost in her parents' tales of the past, certain the KGB were about to drag her away. She'd be locked up forever in a prison cell every bit as authentic as the cheerful boulevard was fake.

"Yes, Mrs. Schmidt?"

"Please bring each of us a refill right away, Erick," Mrs. Schmidt said, her voice clear and steady. "My sister and I will be taking a walk to continue our conversation."

Erick raised his eyebrows and looked at Maria, as if she had any sort of authority or choice in this matter. She nodded, smiling and hoping Mrs. Schmidt didn't notice.

"Right away, Mrs. Schmidt."

The older woman leaned toward Maria, one carefully drawn-on eyebrow raised.

"Perhaps you should tell me who you really are," she said in Romanian, her eyes flashing. "And how you knew to ask me or anyone else about this."

Maria switched to the language of her birth as well.

"I don't mean to offend you or make you uncomfortable, Mrs. Schmidt."

"The only thing that would offend me is if you try to lie to me again," she said with a ghost of a smile. "I know I'm confused sometimes. I know you're not Dorina now. I have time yet before I forget everything about who I am or what I've done. And if we're to talk about such things, I insist you tell me your real name. I won't blow your cover if you're being sincere."

Magda looked away when Erick returned with two small cups, and Maria was relieved to have a break from that intense gaze. Any doubts she had about talking to the wrong person were fading away. Early dementia or not, Mrs. Schmidt had the same penetrating stare as Igor back in her mother's village. She'd always felt undressed, violated somehow, when that man looked at her.

"Enjoy your walk," Erick said. "Just let us know if you need anything, Mrs. Schmidt."

Magda nodded as she got to her feet as smoothly as if she were in her twenties instead of her seventies. She stared down at Maria, her lips pressed together.

"My name is Maria," she said. Sweat trickled down her back under the itchy wool. "Maria Mullins, but I was born Inesceu."

Magda nodded sharply before she walked away. Maria jumped to her feet, nearly knocking the table over in her rush to catch up.

"Erick thinks I'll forget about this clever little buzzer of theirs," Magda said, brushing her fingers across her necklace. It looked like a large ruby surrounded by sapphires. "If I live long enough, I certainly will. For now, though, you have something you need to explain to me."

Maria sipped the too-hot espresso, her mind racing. This window of clarity might not last long. Even more importantly, she didn't want to offend Magda or convince her to report back to Erick or Igor or someone else. She'd read enough tales and seen enough photos to at least put on a convincing act.

"I've just come from a visit to my family's village," she said. "They'd held a funeral right before I arrived, and everyone was upset about how the grave looked. I'd never heard of such things. I started asking questions."

"How did it look, Maria?"

"Like something tunneled its way out," Maria said, still disturbed by the images Paul found. "Like it erupted out of the ground."

Magda walked several steps before she spoke again.

"Do you know if the problem was dealt with?"

"The man I spoke to said they sent it to the second death," Maria said. "I wasn't sure what he meant, but he's growing too old and frail to protect anyone. We need young people to understand, don't we?"

"That has always been the worry," Magda said. They walked down the middle of the broad sidewalk, staying away from everyone else. "We had such a problem under Ceaușescu, with so many dying. We hoped one day to end this plague, to never have to explain it to another generation."

"Maybe we can be the last," Maria said.

"Did the one you spoke to tell you how they dealt with the strigoi?" Magda said.

Maria closed her eyes, chills as painful as burns racing across her flesh. Every time she read or heard that, cold sank deeper into her bones. Maybe she herself was the last.

She picked the first method she'd read about.

"They tracked it to the house it was sheltering in," she said. "Where it was born, I believe. They burned it down."

"Very good," Magda said. "If they poisoned the grave when they saw what happened, that would have been the next place it went. One reason we haven't told your generation much is we don't want to warn the beasts. If one dies ignorant and becomes strigoi despite our best efforts, it will be far easier to catch and put to the second death."

"Where can they shelter?" Maria said. "I was surprised it could go anywhere besides back to the grave."

"The grave is strongest," Magda said. "The safest place to end it is in the earth, after it is poisoned. But the clever ones know anywhere the living person held sacred gives some protection." She raised the hand not holding her tea for a second, as if to cross herself. "Except in a church. Older power holds sway there."

Maria composed herself, drawing upon calm she needed for hostile cross-examinations. She was an expert at hiding how much she knew in order to learn more. Her guilt at taking advantage of a woman with impaired judgment was no match for her desperate need to know why her mother had maimed her body so long ago.

Or why people kept telling her about the undead.

"I hope to keep my village safe, Magda, perhaps bring this plague to an end. I don't want your years of hard work to be in vain. Would you help me? Explain this to me and tell me what to do?"

"I wish we'd spoken when I was younger," she said, touching Maria's arm through the itchy fabric. "I'm more clear today than most, but I fear I'll leave vital things out. Do you have others you can turn to?"

"I do." Maria could only see Paul's face, and Leo's. She hoped neither would ever know what she was doing. "A few people my age are seeking out the remaining ones who know how to fight the strigoi."

"Then I will do my best," Magda said. She stopped and took Maria's free hand. "I will tell you everything I remember, if you promise you will lead the way in ending our horrible curse forever."

"I promise you I'll do everything I can to honor what you tell me today."

Chapter 13

Four years ago

Maria dropped her bag on the sparkling black granite kitchen counter and stood still, listening to their empty house ticking and shifting around her as the air conditioner kicked on.

Leo always kept the place too damned cold, and she'd given up asking him to adjust the thermostat when he went out. With him left to his own devices for two days while she was away, the room was cold enough that her hands and feet ached with the chill.

The last resort Chicago doctor's words still echoed inside her head, chasing her thoughts into muddled storm clouds.

Third surrogate pregnancy failed. All options exhausted.

Further attempts a waste of money and time unless you consider an egg donor. Otherwise, focus on something else. Move on and let it go.

Let it go.

The Gypsy woman, the only one to see and understand what was wrong, had refused to help. Maria's curse, whatever it was, was a part of her. The curse *was* her.

Poor addled Magda never refused to talk to Maria, somehow remembering their conversations even when she thought Maria was her sister. Nothing she'd learned about how to kill a strigoi was going to help her.

Paul was right. She'd made a terrible mistake contacting the old woman.

She wiped a stray tear from her face, her fingertips already numb. Maria's eternally empty stomach growled, the breakfast skipped out of anxiety calling. She opened the right-hand door of the stainless steel refrigerator and grabbed a cup of yogurt, filling her mental grocery list as she scanned the shelves. She leaned down to check the bottom and flinched back, dropping the cup on the white tile floor.

There.

Back in a lost corner of the cavernous fridge, where bottles and jars disappeared for weeks and sometimes months at a time despite their best efforts. The familiar clear glass bottle with black lettering.

Her favorite tonic water. Maria took a step back, shaking her head.

No, she hadn't left one. Not a single one. She hadn't touched one or looked at that part of the store for ten years. Hell, she hadn't had tonic water since before they'd bought this house with room for children who would never exist.

Leo must have bought that while she was gone, thoughtlessly leaving it for her to find on this exact day. Maria let the door swing closed and sat on one of the black leather barstools, gripping the bar that matched the black counters and turning the chair so she could look out the window and try to distract herself.

Her mouth watered and her jaw ached, her nose somehow driving the craving more than any other part of her.

He tried, he always had, but Leo never truly understood her cravings. Not just for booze, either. He'd quit drinking when she did, at least around her. So easy for him, without any kind of struggle. She appreciated that, and many of her AA buddies were envious of support they rarely got from their partners.

But somewhere deep down, Maria wondered if he quit just to show her how easy it was. For him. And that tiny part of her resented him even though it didn't make a damned bit of sense to her sober, rational mind. She kept that part to herself.

He'd never understood her desire for a baby either. One she made with him, not one they adopted. Maria kept her reasons, her true reasons, for that need to herself as well. She pressed her palms flat against the ice-cold granite.

Leo would never understand the awkwardness of other little girls playing with dolls, innocently asking how many children she wanted to have before they'd ever started kindergarten here in the US.

Maria only once said her Mommy told her she couldn't have any. The confusion and even fear in the other girls was too much.

Well-meaning teachers in health and sex ed classes talked about ways to prevent an accidental pregnancy, but never said a word about what to do if you grew up knowing you would never have that worry. Or that choice.

Their friends and even Leo's family were always polite but relentless in the beginning, asking when they were going to add to the grandchildren and cousins. He must have talked to them eventually, after he caught the pained look she couldn't hide any longer.

The questions stopped from people they knew over the years. Even now, strangers never tired of such a hurtful invasion of her privacy. She'd never decided if smugly saying she'd change her mind when she got older was better or worse than a disapproving head shake, or saying she'd regret it eventually.

A few times, though she knew she was angry at the wrong person, Maria said she already regretted it. She said she regretted it every single day, and thanked them so much for reminding her of the option she'd never had.

At least that ended the endless stream of questions and unsolicited advice.

"I'll just go do the shopping," she said, wiping at her cheeks as she got to her feet. "I'll go out, do the shopping, walk around a little bit and get warm. By the time I get back, Leo will be home."

She pulled her phone out and opened their shared grocery list. If Leo happened to be looking at his phone, he'd see the changes. Maybe he'd even realize she was back a day early. Maybe he'd come home in time.

Maria didn't stop long enough to ask herself what he'd come home in time for. Or why she hadn't bothered to let her husband know she was home a day early.

The freezer and all of the cabinets were as well-stocked as the refrigerator, but Maria kept looking. She opened the narrow door of an awkward pantry neither of them ever bothered using, not much more than an excuse to add it to the real estate listing.

The space was out of the way beyond the washer and dryer, and so narrow she had to turn her shoulders sideways to get into it. Even tiny shelves wedged into the long room didn't make this a useful space. Especially not with one dusty light bulb barely reaching a few feet in.

Maria stared into that empty pantry for a long time, conversations blaring through her mind.

They all asked the same questions. The doctors, the healers, even Ana and Paul.

What does Leo think?

What does Leo feel?

Oh sure, they asked about her, but she knew what the real question was. Leo was healthy. Leo was normal. He wouldn't go through all of this, poking and prodding and jerking off into a cup over and over again, if it didn't matter to him.

He wouldn't spend so much money and see doctor after doctor unless he wanted children even worse than she did.

Maria could imagine many things, too many things by far. But she couldn't see herself sitting with Leo and another woman on one of those absurd sofas, the woman carrying Leo's baby. A baby Maria had nothing to do with making.

He'd be better off with a healthy woman, a normal woman, than trying to pretend Maria was either.

Rummaging through the spotless half-bath on this level didn't help any more than inspecting the kitchen had. She knew the upstairs bathrooms wouldn't be out of a damned thing, either.

Leo was his usual logical and organized self, even when she was gone. Even when she didn't want him to be. The three items on the list, yogurt, potatoes, and polenta, hardly seemed worth making a trip.

Her thoughts hardly seemed worth thinking, not when they tore through her brain like jagged bits of metal. Maria had thought enough for a lifetime.

Time to put an end to thinking.

Time to let Leo get on with his own life.

Maria added limes to the bottom, deciding an organic market three towns over would be the best place to find fruit and everything else she needed rather than any of their usual stops closer by. More intrusive questions about whatever she happened to buy wouldn't make a damned thing better. Nor would a clueless—or gossipy—friend telling Leo what Maria bought.

She grabbed her purse and headed back out into the mid-afternoon heat.

Chapter 14

A month ago

THE TRANSPARENT GLASS doors of the hospice ward lurched as Leo passed under the oval black sensor on the pale blue wall above his head, his body breaking the tiny red spot of light on the speckled dusky gray linoleum floor. Before his stride carried him into a skull-cracking impact with the glass, a feat he'd been trying to manage for the last several weeks of this waking nightmare, the doors slid open with a reluctant sigh.

The floor inside was broken with an unyielding line of dark blue tiles. Every time Leo stepped into this too carefully antiseptic hall, he felt a hook deep in his guts, a hook that had responded to Maria since the first time he saw the endless pools of her clear emerald green eyes. Now that internal catch, built into his flesh long enough to feel like part of his elemental DNA, was connecting him to a dead woman without sense enough to stop breathing.

A thrill of anticipation, a jolt of nausea, as if he were at the bottom of the big hill on a wooden roller coaster and the slow ascent just kicked in, drew Leo forward. A scrawny young man with an aggressive crew cut slouched over the growling floor polishing machine. His puke green wrinkled uniform shirt flapped around his thighs. A round cap with Tranquility Gardens embroidered in cheerful orange lettering was shoved to the back of his head. A bright silver nose ring clashed with the cheap fake gold studs shoved through every surface of his ears.

The kid gave a strange backward nod, thrusting his chin into the air to acknowledge Leo's reluctant, shuffling march toward his wife's eventual deathbed. Leo nodded in return, a simple recognition of someone who was there for a paycheck. Not because someone the kid loved more than his own life had grown tired of living.

Leo counted his steps, his shiny black work shoes squeaking on the floor the kid had polished clean. Twenty-five steps brought him to Mr. Evans' room, decorated from floor to ceiling with the yellow and black pennants, posters, and stuffed animals of some football team back East. Mr. Evans' daughter Joyce had been the first person to make an effort to talk to Leo. Her simple greetings reminded him that even though he was here visiting a breathing corpse, he wasn't quite ready to cross the line himself. Not yet.

Joyce Evans-Robinson sat like she always did. Book open on her lap, one hand on her father's wrist, staring out the window at the parking lot. Her father's flesh was thin as dark brown gauze covering a naked bone. When Leo knocked, Joyce jumped before she smiled.

"Leo. How's it going?"

That was one of the unspoken rules in this temple of the dying. You didn't ask how the resident was. Only how the person who might somehow manage to survive was holding up.

"I'm hanging in there," he said, then he held out a small pink paper bag with braided grass handles. "One of my clients brought this by. Thought you might like it."

The grey-haired woman raised one eyebrow as she took the bag. She drew out a gold foil box with a clear plastic top. Nine elaborate chocolates snuggled down inside.

"You devil," she said, shaking her head. Leo saw tears at the corners of her eyes. "You know I don't need any such thing."

"Yeah, none of us do," Leo said, looking back over his shoulder with the biggest smile he could manage. It barely curved his lips. "But sometimes that's not the question. Take care."

That chocolate had cost more than he paid for his own food all day long these days, and he'd gone far out of his way to the best chocolatier in Los Angeles to get it. But Mr. Evans hadn't done a damned thing to end up here except keep breathing for just over a hundred years. His daughter, rail thin and hollow-eyed with mourning, would eat that chocolate if nothing else.

Forty-six steps further along the blue tile line, Leo stopped outside the closed door to the last room on the left. The room that held someone who'd spent the last four years doing everything she could to end up here before either of them turned fifty. Everything she could to twist a dull knife deep into his heart and guts. She didn't quite love him enough to kill him instead.

The nobility and peace he saw in Mr. Evans' daughter waiting by his side eluded Leo, mocked him even though he knew Joyce would die herself before doing such a thing on purpose. All Leo found in this hall, the pine-scented cleaner too close to the goddamned juniper in his nose, was disgust laced with regret.

Chapter 15

One week ago

LEO NEVER HAD a chance to say goodbye to Joyce Evans-Robinson. She said goodbye to her father in the middle of the night, and all evidence of either of them vanished before Leo's next visit. The sadness of not seeing his deathwatch friend hurt: a sharp contrast to the dull ache of sorrow he lived with every moment.

That room surely had new occupant in such a well-regarded facility, but Leo never bothered finding out. He simply passed by the door that was always closed now, just like Maria's. He took care never to look in any of the narrow windows in those anonymous doors.

A wide black fabric belt embroidered with red and blue flowers covered the window in Maria's, more for Leo's continually breaking heart than for his wife. By the time she'd transferred to this ward, she didn't care any more for her privacy or dignity than she did for her life. He'd brought the belt anyway, a cherished reminder of a trip to Prague when his first big client returned a favor by bringing both of them to a movie location.

The staff hadn't argued with him. He knew as well as they did that they'd simply open the door. His wife was past the days of opening doors for herself. Leo didn't bother with the fake smile that caused both of them so much pain in the beginning.

The hospital bed was raised but Maria was asleep, head lolled to the side, mouth open. Leo hardly knew the woman he'd fallen in love with when he was barely twenty years old. Her formerly thick, shining brown hair was thin and brittle. Her full cheeks and mouth wasted as a woman twice her age. Irregular brown spots, stigmata of her dying liver, decorated the yellowish flesh of her hands and forehead. He wondered, not for the first time, if he would even recognize her without the room number to guide him.

Maria had a private room, a benefit of Leo's obsession with having more insurance than they needed. He'd done his best to hide the pale green walls for a couple of weeks. She'd finally shouted that she didn't want this to look like home, so he'd taken almost everything away.

A group of photos of the two of them, taken every year, still hung on the wall beside her. He didn't have the heart to take that away. She'd never mentioned it. Leo didn't think she'd looked at it for a long time, either.

Two reclining chairs that converted into meager beds sat under the window and a small flat-panel TV hung on the wall, but other than that the room was empty. Leo sat in the chair closest to the bed. He watched his wife's wasted chest rise and fall. Rise and fall.

She'd let him promise her, back when he was still convincing himself this was a temporary stay, that he'd never leave without waking her. Leo knew it had been his idea all along, but now he thought of breaking that promise for the first time. The weariness he saw in Joyce Evans-Robinson's face as she waited for her father to die seemed to have replaced all of Leo's own bones and muscles.

He hadn't expected Joyce to escape her obligations to this place before he escaped his.

Before he could make a choice, decide whether to break his promise to a woman who'd broken so many to him, the door opened again. The head nurse's bright cartoon-patterned scrubs broke the somber quiet of the room before he said a word.

"Hey Leo, good to see you," Dan said, as if he didn't see Maria's soon-to-be-widower almost every night.

"You too, Dan. She looks a little out of it. Early pain meds tonight?"

The tall, slender man picked up Maria's chart, running a finger down the list of medications and notes.

"No, nothing special. Her pulse is a bit slower over the last couple of days. That's why I'm checking on her now, but we know that's going to happen. She might just be taking a nap. She'll have to wake up in an hour for her bath if you want to wait."

Leo shook his head. Whether Maria cared or not, he'd learned early on that he couldn't tolerate seeing her so weak she needed a sponge bath.

The one thing she'd refused was to let him bathe her. Watching someone else do what she'd denied him was more than he could handle.

"I'd just be in the way," Leo said.

Dan nodded and reached for Maria's wrist, pale white but nearly as thin as Mr. Evans' had been. Her eyes fluttered open before he raised his watch.

"Hello, beautiful," Dan said. "I'll get out of your hair in a second. That handsome man of yours is much better company than I am."

Leo's heart twisted at the blank expression on his wife's face. Her eyes, yellow around the green and sunken since he'd seen her the night before, were just as empty when she looked into his.

"This is Leo, sweetheart," Dan said, gently putting her hand down and patting it before he made a note on her chart. "Your husband."

Maria stared for several more seconds, seconds that felt like an eternity, before she squeezed her eyes closed. She held out her hand and Leo took it.

"I'm sorry, baby," she said. "I was sleeping pretty hard."

Dan gave a lopsided, sympathetic smile as he stepped out the door.

"I'm like that most of the time whether I've been asleep or not. Let me know if you need anything."

"Don't apologize," Leo said. "I'm sorry to wake you."

He held her cold hand as carefully as he could in both of his, not wanting to bruise the nearly exposed bones. She hated to be cold. Her flesh always was now.

"You promised me, remember?" she said. "I have friends who will make sure it holds up in court if you sneak out of here."

"You're right," Leo said, kissing the tissue thin skin between her thumb and fingers. "I won't forget."

"Listen, I need to tell you something. This new drug they've got me on is knocking me out longer and longer."

"I'll tell Dan," Leo said. "I'm sure he can adjust it."

"No, baby." Maria moved her head slowly against the pillow. "It's for the pain. The only way he can adjust it is up, and not much further. I want to be buried in Transylvania, where my father is."

Leo blinked, then scowled before he could stop himself. Talk of death wasn't especially surprising at this stage, at least not according to everything he'd read. But this was.

"I thought you wanted to be here, by the ocean."

"I did. I do," she said. "But I need to be there. My whole family is there in that village, Leo, going back longer than anyone knows. I feel it more and more the closer I get."

"I'm not there," Leo said.

He knew it was selfish. For once, he didn't care.

"No, and I don't want you to be," Maria said. "Not while you're still alive. I don't want my only family that matters spending the rest of his life visiting a bunch of bones in the ground. If you insist on going to Romania once in a while, I guess I can't stop that. But I don't want you wasting time over me."

The molecule thin layer of frost that protected Leo, kept him from falling to pieces from the second he woke up alone to the second he got back into bed alone, fractured under the strain. His confusion and rage and agony, so firmly confined to that lonely bed, nearly pushed him into screaming at the person he so desperately wanted to protect from it.

"I'm not wasting time if I'm spending it with you," he said through a tight throat. "I'll decide when my time is wasted."

"While I'm alive, you're right," she said, squeezing his hand harder than he thought she could. "But that won't last much longer. You're not dying, Leo. I am. I'm running out of choices just as much as I'm running out of heartbeats. You need to respect this one. And do everything they say, no matter how strange it might sound to you. Promise me."

Leo watched her, thinking of her doctor's last words. Her final doctor, the one who was tasked with sending her as easily as possible into death. Not months, probably not even weeks. This woman he couldn't remember not loving, spending as much time as he possibly could with, was leaving him.

He could yell and scream and sob over that all he wanted to, but never around her. After she was gone, it wouldn't matter anymore. He wasn't about to waste any of his remaining time arguing with her.

"All right, Maria. I'll make sure of it. I promise."

Chapter 16

Five days ago

LEO CLOSED his eyes and rubbed at his forehead, not quite aware that the spot matched Maria's deep scar. He wished he could push a button and make everything and everyone slow down around him, then edit the scene like a movie.

The long, airy meeting room at the Transylvanian village inn was big enough for at least twenty people, more than twice the number sitting at the round table with him. High windows tilted open at the top lined three of the stone walls, the warm spring breeze at odds with the frozen thing in his chest.

"I'm sorry, Ana, I'm not following," Leo said to the woman next to him.

He'd known her more than half his life, but even she wasn't making sense to him right now. Everyone at the table had paper in front of them. Only Leo's was blank. Ana smiled sadly, patted his back, then leaned forward and started talking in much faster Romanian.

Two black-robed priests sat across from them, along with Maria's mother and two fragile but intimidating old women from the village. All wore black mourning headscarves. They were joined by a middle-aged man who was some sort of leader. Leo couldn't tell if Igor was anything as formal as a mayor, but even the priests glanced at him for approval from time to time.

He'd never been as fluent in Romanian as he'd wanted, and now he barely understood a word.

His command of English hadn't been much better since the doctor told him his wife's heart beat no longer.

Ana nodded at the two old women, then turned to Leo. Her waves of long, dark blonde hair glinted in the sunlight, and her round, open face was made for far more pleasant expressions. Right now her brow was knotted and her mouth drawn tight.

"They say her burial here is okay as long as their traditions are followed," Ana said, her accent a softer, warmer version of a Russian's. "The flight keeps them from watching the body properly. As long as everything else is correct, they will let it pass."

"Watching the body? What do they want?" Leo said, then whispered. "Maria never liked any of this. She thought it was all superstition."

"Sometimes ideas of superstition change when we get older," Ana said. "I'm sorry, but you did tell me she wanted to be laid to rest here. She said that right before she passed, did she not?"

Leo tilted his head to the side and closed his eyes. His love had told him again minutes before her last breath. Whispers he would never have believed true if she hadn't said the same thing a few days before.

"Yes," he said, his voice rough and low, his gut churning. "After years of telling me she wanted no part of this. Apparently she hid a lot more than drinking from me."

"I'm truly sorry, Leo. All of us have broken hearts, but yours the worst of all. Do we need to wait and discuss this another time?"

Leo looked at the dark logs spanning the ceiling for a few seconds, wanting nothing more in that moment than to keep himself from crying in front of the friends and strangers alike. Igor stared at Leo with his arms crossed, wearing a brown polo shirt and khaki pants but with the attitude of an expensive suit and tie. All of it was a strange contrast to the man's unshaven stubble, a mark of respect to the dead.

"We don't have another time, Ana," Leo said. "She'll be here tonight. Just tell me what they want."

"You've been to funerals here before," Ana said. "You know about her fir tree, the songs. You don't have to worry about the food and things like that. Everything will be at her auntie's house, and Elena will handle it."

Leo looked at his mother-in-law and tried to smile, hoping it wasn't too much of a grimace. He hadn't spoken to Elena since that terrible phone call from the hospice ward. Breaking the news that her daughter was dead. The older woman nodded, dabbing at her eyes with the corner of her scarf.

Ana startled him by speaking again. "'The Song of the Dawn' will be in the morning as if she'd died overnight. We normally wait for two days, but her funeral will be tomorrow afternoon. Will you be ready?"

"As I can be," Leo said. "Do I need to bring anything?"

Ana turned her notes so Leo could see them. She'd written neat English translations below her scrawling Romanian.

"You already have her clothing ready," she said. "And we'll have the bread for her journey." She tapped one line with her pen. "Would you like me to bring the *pălincă*?"

"*Pălincă*?" Leo blinked, certain he'd misunderstood, but that same word was written on the page. "Why the hell would I bring alcohol? That's what killed her."

"No, not to drink, not for us," she said, patting Leo's hand. "This is to bury with her. A very old family and village tradition."

"No," Leo said, shaking his head. "I won't do that."

Everyone in the room started talking to each other in quiet Romanian, except for Igor. He only stared at Leo.

"This is part of what they insist on, especially since they could not watch the body," Ana said, glancing at the three women. All of them crossed themselves repeatedly. "Everyone buried in the village has the same."

"That's too damned bad," Leo said, pushing his chair back. The metal legs screeched on the stone floor. "She killed herself with booze, Ana. You know that. I'm not putting her into the ground with it. No."

She stood when he did, grasping his forearm before speaking to the others in the room. Leo didn't bother trying to catch any of her words. It didn't matter. He took a deep breath, forcing his brain to slow down enough to drag a few words of Romanian out of cold storage.

"Thank you for your time," he said. "I apologize for causing trouble, but I won't agree..."

The horrified look in his mother-in-law's eyes ground his words, and his mind, to a halt. Maria hadn't spoken to her for several years after some kind of fight. She'd never told Leo the reason, but he didn't want to hurt his mother-in-law any more than losing her only child had. Whatever he had to do to put a stop to this nonsense, he'd do without dragging Maria's mother through anything more.

Leo turned and walked out. Ana kept pace with two steps for every one of his. An ancient mama dog lay on the black stones in the middle of the courtyard, only her eyes following them.

"Leo, please, it will all be okay."

"Look, I know you're trying to help, Ana. I couldn't get through any of this without you. But you didn't see her at the end." He felt himself running out of breath as his words went faster, and he couldn't do a damned thing to stop it. "You didn't see her waste away and bloat up at the same time. You didn't see her eyes and her skin turn yellow. You didn't see the liver spots. Liver spots, and she wasn't even fifty fucking years old! My wife killed herself with that stuff, and I won't put her under the ground with that same shit!"

Leo winced at the sound of his own voice echoing off the four walls around them. The dog raised her head. No one else had come out, but he was quite sure they could hear.

"I'm sorry, Ana," he said, meaning to step toward her. "I just want this to be over."

He staggered, maybe tripping on a ridge of stone. Maybe losing the strength in his legs. Ana caught him and held tight. Leo let out a groaning, painful breath he'd been holding for days, a breath made more of tears than air.

He was terrified he'd never draw another.

He was terrified he'd keep breathing after all.

"No, I'm the one who's sorry," Ana whispered close to his ear.

"You're here all alone without your Maria, and I'm letting them put you through all of this."

"She can't be gone," Leo whispered, forcing the words through his throat. "I can't breathe without her."

"Your heart will keep beating even when it's shattered, my friend. All our hearts keep beating. You don't believe me now, and you don't have to, but finally someday you'll notice you feel a tiny bit better."

Chapter 17

Silence was good.

Silence was what she'd needed for months. Years, really. If everything would just stop moving and shifting around her, she would sleep for years now. Maybe then she'd wake up and everything would be normal again.

Still.

Be still!

She couldn't quite find her way to her voice, and the motion never stopped. Maybe Leo could help her, at least keep her warm so the changes and adjustments wouldn't be so awful. She couldn't remember ever being so cold.

Leo had to be close by, she could almost feel him. Not quite smell or hear, but the same echo of her soul and his that she'd felt for half her life.

Almost.

But that wasn't good enough.

She tried to get close to him, to find that connection. The space inside where she fit.

Something wasn't right. Like one lone flute out of tune in a massive orchestra, some small thing was out of place. The size didn't matter, not here. One thing off kept everything from working.

Heat rose up in her, warmth that was uncomfortable and angry and too big to stay in one place, even if she wanted it to. The heat was orange, red, tinged with black.

For the first time in her life, a warm thing leaving her felt better than clutching at it for all she was worth.

The movement continued no matter how she wished it to stop, willed it, demanded it. Pushing the hot energy out, finding more and more places to send it to, helped more than she thought it would.

Cool moved in, even though calm did not. That was good enough for now. She would find Leo and be safe again.

Chapter 18

Four days ago

A SLAMMING car door jerked Leo out of a fitful sleep, stiff muscles making him wonder where he was for several seconds. Outside, cool and damp in the early evening, sprawled awkwardly on a wooden swing. Someone closed a sliding door on a van in the gravel driveway beside him.

He finally recognized the neat yard when he heard Costel's deep, booming voice. The tall, rangy man passed right by Leo as he talked to the driver. A smaller figure carrying a travel bag started toward the inn, then detoured into the yard.

"How you doing, big brother?"

Leo smiled, the first time in longer than he could remember it being true and honest.

"Better now that you're here, Bri."

Brian dropped the bag and met Leo in a hug hard enough to crack his spine.

"You're covered with dew," Brian said. "What are you doing, sleeping out here?"

"Fell asleep waiting on you." Leo grabbed the bag and both men started toward the inn. "You hungry?"

"Too jetlagged to eat," Brian said. "Don't tell Mom, she'll think I'm...never mind. That reminds me, they both send their best, wish they could make it. You know the routine. I'll make up for skipping dinner in the morning."

"Costel would be happy to stuff you senseless," Leo said. "Mom would be relieved to know there's always more than enough to eat around here. Maria...we both used to bitch about gaining weight after every trip."

Brian stopped and put a hand on Leo's shoulder. They shared the same wavy brown hair. Leo's normally corporate neat, but at the moment it brushed his collar like his kid brother's always had. The same light brown eyes looked into his from their mother's round face rather than the long features of their father that Leo saw in the mirror.

"Over the phone isn't good enough for this," Brian said. "I'm so sorry, man. This isn't fair."

"No, it's not," Leo said. "I appreciate you bringing her more than you know. She would too."

They walked up the steep, black stone staircase together. Leo opened the third door on the left with the key Costel had given him before he fell asleep. The rustic room seemed larger than his with only the single bed, and sheer curtains floated in the breeze from the open balcony door.

"No one on either side of you," Leo said. "So you'll be able to get some sleep if you didn't on the plane. The firm got you first class, didn't they?"

Brian tossed the bag on the floor and sat heavily on the bed.

"Great service, shitty sleep. Not the airline's fault. I usually sleep like a baby on flights, even crammed into coach. Nothing but weird dreams this time, though. The whole plane seemed restless. I don't think anyone slept, ten thousand dollar seats or not."

"Well, you'll make up for it tonight," Leo said. "Might want to close that balcony door before you crash. Don't want to invite Dracula in."

Brian snorted before he leaned over to pull his tennis shoes off.

"Maria might not be able to hear you," he said. "But from what I remember, her mother can still take you out. Soon as I brush my teeth, I'll be out too. See you in the morning."

Leo closed the door and walked up the rough wooden stairs to his room, the one he'd shared with his wife on many previous visits. After seeing the space in Brian's room, his seemed even more cramped with the double bed, but he didn't mind. Masochistic or pathetic, he wanted everything the same. He stepped out onto the small balcony in time to see the van backing out of the long driveway.

He'd made sure not to glance inside, and he was grateful to Brian for not saying anything about the cargo. He knew Maria was on her last trip. The van that brought her from Bucharest would take her a mile or so further on to the tiny, beautiful church, and tomorrow afternoon she'd be with her family.

Her family that wasn't him.

The van turned onto the main road and drove out of sight, but Leo stayed where he was.

He didn't want to fight with Ana or anyone else over the damned booze in his wife's coffin, and he hoped he wouldn't have to. If he was careful, and quick, he'd get his way and everyone would rest easy believing the traditions had been followed.

Leo went to bed himself, hoping this one night would let him rest easy as well. The rest of his life was time enough for nightmares.

Chapter 19

ALL WAS STILL AT LAST. And yet there was no peace.

She had no pain, none of the discomfort that she'd lived with for so long. But the longing was deep. The longing overwhelmed every part of her and worsened with every passing second.

Leo was the key, as he had been and always would be.

She pushed, strained, and she put herself into motion. Not hurtling, too fast and cold and out of control. She moved deliberately now. She felt him drawing her, pulling her near. Going to Leo was the easiest thing in a world grown far more easy.

Staying away was the terrible effort.

One place after another, no need to touch. What she needed was not there. But the faint light and warmth grew, and she continued on.

A familiar space, one she knew as well as she knew her own shape and sound. A space she'd returned to many times.

There. There!

She drifted down, more gently than fog over the grass, and settled where she belonged more than anywhere else. This warmth and safety was all she ever needed, far more than crude air or water.

Home at last, she slept.

Chapter 20

Three days ago

THE DRIFTING, eerie sound of alpenhorns pulled Leo out of the deepest sleep he'd had for longer than he could remember. He knew those were for Maria, for her funeral later that day. The old women who'd been there for the arrangements would be singing "The Song of the Dawn" for her before much longer. The finality unnerved him even more than the doctor's words back in the hospice ward had.

Some part of him, maybe his heart, had been lonely and cold since she moved out of their house to finish her slow suicide. He didn't think that would ever change as long as he lived, no matter what Ana said.

That part felt safe and warm this morning even though he couldn't remember a single dream.

He slid the door open and stepped out onto the balcony like he'd done every morning for so many years, every time they stayed in this inn. The sun was barely lighting the valley, but it was already warmer than during the night. A sharp temperature drop had overcome Leo's dislike of sleeping in a closed-in room.

The chickens were stirring around even ahead of the rooster waking up or the girl coming out to take their eggs. Nothing else was moving yet except an old mama dog. Like she had the last few days, she paced around the yard, sitting for a few minutes, then moving to another spot. She didn't seem hurt, just restless. He hoped she was only feeling the chill from the night before and not getting sick with something. For the first time since he'd arrived, none of the other dogs were hanging around with her.

Another door slid open, and Brian stepped out onto the balcony below wearing a pair of shorts and nothing else. He looked pale and too thin in the faint light. Leo was surprised to see a bald spot high on his brother's head, one he had no signs of himself, at least not yet. Lurking up here waiting for the younger man to scratch or fart would be a rotten way to start a difficult day.

"Hope I didn't wake you," he said, trying not to wake anyone else. Brian hunched his shoulders and looked up, then smiled.

"Shit, I didn't see you up there. No, I've been awake for a while. How do you sleep through all those dogs barking?"

"I didn't hear a thing," Leo said, glancing out at the mama dog. "They usually say good morning, but not 'til a little later."

"Well, they never shut up." Brian yawned, squeezing his eyes closed. "All night long. You must have been sleeping like the...like a rock. What time will breakfast be ready? I'm over that much of my jet lag."

"Couple of hours," Leo said. "There's always stuff left over from yesterday. Meet me downstairs in five and I'll make you some coffee. Long day coming."

Neither man spoke until both of them had finished their first cup, a lifelong habit and understanding. Leo watched his brother tear into the pastries, somehow better than what he got anywhere else even a day old. He wondered if he'd ever be here again to enjoy them. The thought of never coming back hurt, but he wasn't sure if returning by himself with Maria in the ground less than a mile away would be easier or harder.

"All right, I may make it through the rest of the day now," Brian said, pouring more coffee for both of them. "Or at least until breakfast. What can I do to help you out today?"

Leo rubbed his face with both hands and sighed, his coffee-scented breath hot against his skin.

"Getting me away from here would probably be the kindest thing," he said. "Short of that, just make sure I don't make an asshole of myself."

"I don't think anyone would blame you if you did," Brian said. "Seriously, let me know, okay? I've never been to a funeral here, but I've been to enough to get the general idea."

"The only thing I may need help with is getting some time alone," Leo said. He finally knew how to deal with the pălincă in the coffin. "With her, I mean, right before the service. Chase everyone out and give me a few minutes, maybe?"

"You got it, least I can do. Anything I need to watch out for at the funeral?"

"Not really," Leo said. "It will be a lot longer than you expect, and we'll be standing the whole time. If it's like the other ones I've been to, they'll have a tree there, the one that was supposed to be linked to her. It has to die now too."

Leo thought his voice was calm enough, but something about those words, about the tree being cut down the same way his wife was instead of growing tall and strong on the mountainside, twisted the knife all over again.

Brian closed his eyes and let out his breath. Apparently Leo's voice hadn't been quite as calm as he thought. The young girl walked through the kitchen with her egg basket just then, rescuing him with her cheerful smile.

"Sorry, enough questions from me," Brian said. "I'm not awake enough to keep my own foot out of my mouth. More coffee needed. I'll follow your lead, brother."

Chapter 21

Brian was as good as his word, staying at Leo's side after the endless funeral, stepping in to introduce himself whenever Maria's family got too upset. Or too close. Leo kept himself distracted watching his brother smiling and working the crowd even though he didn't know a single word of Romanian.

So much like their mother at times like this. Better than his big brother was, even after Leo'd spent the last twenty years working with ego-starved celebrities. He knew he wouldn't have made it through the day without Brian's smooth, people-handling interference.

Just as he'd expected, someone had tucked the required bottle of pălincă into the coffin beside his wife. Leo didn't have to ask Ana to suspect it had been Igor, the same one everyone had been seeking approval from when they made these arrangements. The man watched the coffin—and Leo—like some kind of predator throughout the hours of the funeral.

Brian noticed the close observation without Leo saying a word. He recognized the person most likely to help on his own as well. He walked up with Ana as everyone else was at last filing out of the tiny stone church.

"Is that guy some kind of hit man?" Brian said.

"Never saw him before a couple of days ago," Leo said. "Haven't heard him say a word, but everyone pays attention to him. Is he the mayor or something?"

"Igor was high up with the Soviets a long time ago," Ana said. "Not as formal as a mayor." She looked up and to the left, searching for the words. "Now he's more like a historian. He knows the history around here better than anyone teaching at school."

"Leo wants a few minutes alone with her," Brian said to Ana. "Can you help me get Mr. History out of here?"

Ana watched Leo for a few seconds, and he was sure she could see right through him. Not only his intentions, but the water-filled pălincă bottle in his coat pocket. He concentrated on staying calm.

"Just a few," she finally said. "Maybe not minutes. Everyone's jumpy enough already, whether they believe in the old ways or not."

She leaned forward and kissed Leo's cheek, then walked toward Igor. Brian raised his eyebrows.

"Old ways?" Brian said.

"No idea," Leo said, shrugging. "Appreciate the assist."

"No worries, we'll do our best. See you out there."

Leo stood beside the casket, looking anywhere but at his bride's still face. He'd been struggling to avoid seeing her all afternoon. The random glimpses out of the corner of his eye were more than enough. Voices behind him rose for a moment, then slowly moved out the door with the rest. He risked a quick glance behind him to make sure they were all gone.

"I'm sorry, Maria," he whispered, closing his eyes and clenching his fists. He couldn't do this without seeing her, probably without touching her for the last time. "I'm so damned sorry that I never could figure out what you needed. How to help. I'm breaking my last promise to you not a week after I made it. I'm going to have to live with that for the rest of my life. "

He turned his face down and opened his eyes.

At first all he saw was her dark blue dress, primly buttoned all the way to the collar. Her skin was pale and still above it. Leo pulled his fake bottle out and switched it with the one tucked in beside her hip, wincing when it brushed against her arm.

Her flesh didn't yield any more than the padded side of the coffin, as if she'd never breathed or moved her body against his.

Leo's gaze shifted to her face, and he nearly dropped the full bottle. His wife looked more calm and peaceful than she had for a long time. Maybe years. Her skin was too pale and her face a tiny bit puffy, but she'd been worse over the last few months. The liver spots were covered up, and her hair seemed as clean and shiny as when she'd been able to take care of it herself.

Whoever had done this makeup job had even put a lifelike flush of excitement on her cheeks. Her lips were full and red, and Leo surprised himself by leaning down to kiss her.

He would have sworn her lips were warm.

"Goodbye, Maria. I hope you're as peaceful as you look."

He slipped the bottle into his pocket and draped the coat over his arm just in time to hear the comically loud throat clearing behind him. The ghostly tones of women crying out her final mourning song filtered through the door. The old Soviet boss was walking in, the priest and the men who would carry her hard on his heels.

Following these men out, behind Maria's coffin, would be his first steps into a life he'd never wanted.

A life without her.

Chapter 22

Leo was surprised to find himself as ravenous as his brother had been at breakfast after the short walk from the church to the feast. Maria's aunts had helped her mother put out a remarkable amount of food even for the abundant meals he was used to in Transylvania. Specially cured meats, early spring greens and last year's pickles, and the usual mounds of polenta layered with cheese, covered every surface in the neat, small kitchen. He gladly took the excuse, and Brian's assistance, to eat and avoid conversation as much as he possibly could.

He'd offered to pay for at least part of the food, but Maria's relatives had politely declined. Leo suspected, and hoped, that much of the food was provided by neighbors instead of bought by one small family.

He was thinking of trying to escape, to walk back by the graveyard on the way to the inn, when Maria's mother stepped away from the dark-haired young woman she'd been talking to and sat down beside him. Leo saw Brian walking toward him with glasses of water. He shook his head at his brother's startled expression.

"This is a wonderful feast, Elena," Leo said as he turned to Brian. "You remember my little brother?"

"Of course I do," Elena said. Brian kissed both of her cheeks as smoothly as if he'd been born in Europe. "So good to see you again, Brian."

"You too, ma'am, though I wish the situation were different."

"We all do," she said, lowering her eyes for a second. "I need to speak to Leo for a moment."

This time Leo nodded at Brian, who sat the two glasses down before he walked away.

"He's watching over you," Elena said, watching the younger man walk away.

"I don't know what I would have done without him. How are you holding up, Elena?"

"It's a terrible thing, to bury your child," she said. Her voice was steady but tears stood in her eyes. "A heartbreak too many of us here have known in the past. I didn't think it would happen to my Maria."

"No," Leo said. "I didn't either."

"How long will you stay, Leo? In Romania?"

"I have a few more weeks before I have to get back," he said. "I might travel around a little. Try to get my head on straight. Going home isn't going to be easy."

She put her hand on his forearm.

"I'm so very sorry, Leo. I wonder what I did to bring such a weakness into Maria, that she died so young. I did the best I could to protect her, but times were not easy."

"I don't think it was anything you did," Leo said. "No one knows what causes addiction. She had a lot of good years."

Elena shook her head and wiped her eyes with that black handkerchief. Leo didn't understand all the hardness between Maria and her mother. He hoped Elena would be able to get past it on her own.

"It hurt her, not being able to have babies with you," she said. "I had no easy choices back then. I'm not sure I made any of the right ones."

"You raised a strong, wonderful woman," Leo said. He'd believe it himself again someday. "One I fell in love with the second I saw her and stayed in love with for more than half my life. Probably the rest of my life. We can't blame ourselves. That doesn't help anyone."

"She was right to be with you," Elena said, her chin trembling. "I know she loved you until the end, Leo. Thank you for taking care of her. And thank you for letting us take care of her today."

She leaned forward and kissed his cheek, then she was gone. Brian sat down beside him before Leo could catch his breath.

"Everything all right?"

"As good as it can be," Leo said, then he drank half the water. He wished it were the pălincă he still had in his coat. "She hasn't exactly been the most approving mother-in-law in the world. Maria hadn't spoken to her for years, but she wouldn't tell me why."

"Just as well she lives in New York, maybe," Brian said. "Ready to get out of here?"

"Yeah, let's go before she decides to be even more honest. I don't think my heart could take it."

The two men walked slowly toward the door, and several people did indeed embrace Leo. Elena had rejoined the young woman she'd been talking to earlier. Whoever she was, her pale blue eyes followed Leo as they slipped away. Elena only nodded at him.

If he'd known that would be the last time he saw Maria's mother alive, Leo might have endured one last hug.

Chapter 23

Leo made a point of going straight to the awkward upstairs pantry as soon as they returned to the inn, keeping a promise he'd made to himself on the way back. His descent into near madness, and Maria's to her death, started in the cramped and useless space in their house in California. He had to bring some part of it to an end right here.

He stepped inside and pushed the bottles of alcohol back, making room for an extra one. He turned it to match all the pălincă and added it to the supply. He made himself another promise to get rid of each and every bottle of gin hidden in their house in California.

It was his house now, and past time to find something useful to do with the space. Even if he was left with a shallow closet or shelves. Anything but a secret space, a hidden knife waiting to sink into his back with no warning.

Three hours later, just as the sun was setting on the longest day of Leo's life, the innkeeper found him and Brian sitting in the second level courtyard. They'd been talking about anything but Maria for a couple of hours.

Leo caught himself relaxing and enjoying himself, pulling out of the pit in his heart for minutes at a time. He was starting to wonder if he might be able to adjust to being a single man again after all. The same ancient black and brown mama dog he'd seen hanging around the inn since he'd arrived had made her way carefully up the stone steps, the first time Leo had seen her up there. She was lying with her head on his foot when Costel joined them.

"I hope you'll join us for a light supper," Costel said, sitting on the wooden bench beside Leo and scratching the dog's head. "Good company helps after a hard day, and the two of you are very good company. I wish you could stay longer, Brian. The car will be here for you at four in the morning."

"Wish I could stay longer, too, especially with that wake up time. I never thought I'd eat again after stuffing myself this afternoon," Brian said, rubbing his stomach. "But I'm actually hungry. Even in first class, airplane food will be a sad substitute."

"Smart man, my little brother," Leo said. "He already knows you never turn down something Costel cooked. Outside or inside?"

"Outside, yes," the innkeeper said, smiling. "Wonderful warm weather for so early in the spring. I'll see you down there."

The long tables in the outdoor dining room were empty except for Costel, his wife, Brian and Leo. A bottle of pălincă stood at the head of the table with four shot glasses, and Leo knew at once it was the same one he'd pulled out of Maria's coffin. A faint streak of the makeup from her hand still twisted along the side, not completely rubbed off in his pocket.

The last trace of her left in the world.

Leo nearly refused when the tiny glasses were passed along, still caught up in over ten years of habit when offered alcohol with Maria by his side. He laughed under his breath and accepted the offer. He would face countless milestones and changes as he walked into his life as a widower. Some easier, some far harder. He'd never considered making his choices about drinking or not based on his own feelings rather than hers.

And what could be more appropriate and fitting than that first guilt-free drink coming from this bottle, the one meant to be wasted under the ground?

Chapter 24

Motion again. Frantic, seeking motion.

This time under her own power, but with no control.

She was there. That woman was there. The one who scarred and cursed the flesh that was not her own.

The heat was back, too, and she understood. The warmth was fury, and fury was the sustenance she needed. Fury and fear drove her on, gave her the energy to keep searching.

Keep seeking.

The demon rode the nightmares throughout the village until the sun came up and she was forced to rest again.

The thing she needed most eluded her. It would not elude her forever.

Chapter 25

Now

LEO STEPPED onto the graveled driveway outside the inn, letting the heavy glass-paneled door swing closed behind him. The yard was empty, but swirling patterns in the dew on the grass showed how agitated the dogs had been just a few minutes before while Leo watched from his balcony. The mama dog and all her furious offspring must have settled down as soon as the poor mangy stray ran toward the woods.

Only the old brown and black mama dog was still there. She sat at the end of the driveway as if she'd been waiting for him, tapping her foot and staring pointedly at her watch the whole time.

The chickens and bright guinea hens were calm, and the air of menace Leo had felt earlier was gone as well. Whatever the strange shadow moving over the ground had been, it had moved on with the dogs. Or it floated out of Leo's mind once he woke up a little more. He shrugged and walked toward the road.

"Just me this morning, girl," he said. The dog's triangular ears perked up at his voice. "My little brother had to go back home. Want to walk with me?"

She fell into step with Leo just as she had with him and Brian during his visit. The younger man had insisted on walking down to the tiny convenience store several times. Brian claimed it was to get a Coke for his jet lag, but Leo suspected it was just to get him moving and out of his own head. Whatever the reason, the habit felt too good to give up.

They'd seen many people out and about on their walks, but today no one was in any of the yards or driving on the narrow road. With Leo's encouragement, Brian had learned to trust the drivers without jumping into the ditch every time someone passed by. That wasn't a problem this morning. He made it the mile to the store without seeing a single person, or even another dog.

He was relieved to see the door standing open as usual, dispelling his half-serious worries about the world ending while he'd slept so hard. The dog waited outside the door without Leo saying a word. The store was as deserted as the street except for the stooped old man behind the counter. He glanced at Leo, but instead of his usual warm smile and loud greeting, he stared at his hands.

Leo grabbed a couple of bottles of Coke, wondering if something had happened overnight. He had no way to put the empty village and strange behavior together with how the dogs acted that morning. Not yet.

"Good morning," he said, pulling his Romanian money out of his pocket. When he looked up, the man was still focused on his own hands. "That's five lei, right?"

The man never met Leo's gaze or spoke. He took the twenty lei bill and counted out the change. After an awkward few seconds, Leo turned and left. Whatever it was, he didn't feel right prying into a near stranger's business. The dog fell into step beside him again.

"At least you're speaking to me," he said. People were moving around now, but they turned away as he drew near. Some of the older women crossed themselves and went inside. "I'm either missing something or I have a good case of paranoia."

The silence and disappearing act continued until Leo got back to the inn. He scratched the dog's ears, reminding himself to bring her some kind of treat for being nice to him. When he got to the kitchen, breakfast was on the table but the room was empty. He put the Coke in the fridge for later and sat down to eat alone.

"Leo, good morning," Costel said, speaking so quietly that Leo didn't recognize his voice.

"Morning. I'm glad you can see me. I was beginning to have my doubts."

The tall man's brow drew down, but he looked more afraid than confused. He sat across from Leo.

"I can see you," he said, still speaking low. "It has been a strange morning, my friend."

"Yeah, what's going on?" Leo said. "I walked into the village and didn't see much of anyone. The people I did see wouldn't speak or even look at me."

The innkeeper sat forward with his elbows on the table, rubbing the back of his neck.

"Tell me, did you sleep well last night, Leo?"

"I slept very well," Leo said. "Better than I expected to."

"You will be the only one in the whole village, then," Costel said. He poured coffee for himself and topped up Leo's cup. "You mentioned wanting to walk in the woods? This would be a good day for that, I think."

"Wait, what's going on?" Leo said, uneasiness creeping back into his mind.

"It is probably nothing," Costel said. "But when many people have nightmares and trouble sleeping, especially after a funeral, it is best for a stranger to be away. No one will hurt you, Leo. Perhaps this will blow over, though."

"What could I possibly have to do with a bunch of people having a restless night?"

"Let me prepare lunch for you," Costel said, nodding. "And I'll drive you to the trail if you like. It will be cool and sunny today, perfect for a walk."

Leo stared, not sure how he should respond. He was one step behind everything around him.

"Have I done something wrong?"

"No, no," the innkeeper said, but he didn't smile. "Old beliefs are strong here, that's all. When people are uneasy and you want a day to yourself, the time is right to take advantage. I will pack your lunch myself."

"You've got a deal on the lunch," he said. "And the walk sounds good too. As long as you tell me what this belief is. I don't want to spend the whole day looking over my shoulder."

Costel sighed, staring out the window and then into Leo's eyes.

"I have no wish to hurt you, but I don't want you to worry all day. When Andrej went into the village this morning to do our shopping, everyone wanted to talk of their bad nights. Uneasy sleep, bad dreams, waking many times sure they'd heard a noise in the darkness. Andrej passed a hard night himself, and I'm sorry to say this, but so did I. When people have a night like this after a funeral, the old belief is that the soul is restless."

Leo opened and closed his mouth, certain he'd say the wrong thing but unable to say nothing. He surprised himself by speaking his wife's name without a wave of sadness for the first time in weeks.

"They think Maria's come back from the dead?"

"I don't think most people truly believe that, no," Costel said. "Some of the older people may. But they all know the burial was proper, Leo. They know this is not true."

"The burial was proper?" Leo said, his mouth disengaged from his brain. "That's the only reason they know this isn't true, that she's not roaming the countryside?"

To his great relief, Costel laughed. He didn't meet Leo's eyes for a few seconds, though.

"I'm sure you have these things in America," he said. "Where it may not make sense but it's easier to do what the old people want. Yes?"

"Yes. I can't deny that, even if I wanted to." Leo finished his coffee and rubbed his face. "So get me out of sight for the day, let the old folks take a nap, and we'll all feel better tomorrow."

"You understand perfectly," the other man said, getting to his feet. "I'll have your lunch ready in ten minutes."

"Hey, can you pack something for the old mama dog, the brown one? She's the only one who would speak to me this morning until you came down."

Chapter 26

Animals had no space for her now. She was too strong. Too solid. She left the dogs behind and moved out into the forest with the sunrise.

Peace here, far more than she'd known under the ground. Peace, and something soft and familiar. Moving closer, coming toward her.

As always. Through time and space. Coming toward her.

She moved easily, not caring that she brought unease along with her. The creatures were not her concern. What she wanted most would have to wait until she was stronger.

What she needed now lay quiet. Soft. Warm and sleeping. Close enough to touch, if she could only touch.

She focused, concentrated, drew from all the living, moving things around her. Closer. She cast the faintest of shadows, drifted gently across the tumbling water.

One with the water, moving through vibrant deep green, reaching up to the warmth of his body.

The energy vanished in a growling rush.

Shadowy and weak again, she drew back, but not before the wood fell silent. Everything frozen and still. The growl intensified.

The dog knew.

She circled him, keeping away from countless creatures that knew to watch for her now. Wanting to stay but unable.

The dog watched.

He sat up, and she knew his fear. Fear of the silence. Fear of her. That was more than she could bear.

She moved close again, drifting like mist along the ground. Floating to his side. Slipping easily into his flesh, calming his jangled nerves. The risk was terrible with the watcher close by, but his need too great to ignore.

The peace came back to her, threefold, tenfold. Peace and strength she never knew he had filled her. Restored her. Brought her closer to her mind and awareness of what she had to do.

Comforting him gave her more than it took.

She followed as they left, the man and the dog, getting closer whenever she could. The creatures and the dog knew her every time.

The man did too.

She savored his opening, his welcome, like a kiss in the night.

Chapter 27

Leo finally understood his brother's obsession with hiking. The trees were beginning to bloom with a rich, lush color and scent he'd always missed living in LA. He tried to resist the thought, but his eyes and nose brought it home to him over and over again. The forest teemed with growth and new life. The most natural thing in the world, no matter that it made him melancholy and lonely.

Rebirth after a time of dark and stillness.

The same quiet and lack of people that had so unnerved him in the village was soothing out in the woods with the mama dog by his side. No, not quiet. Not really. More birds than he'd heard in years chatted and darted around him. Maybe he only noticed them walking without another person to talk to, but their songs were sweet. Small creatures he never quite caught sight of rustled through the leaves and undergrowth.

His thighs and calves burned with the steady climb and heavy hiking boots he wasn't used to wearing. They were almost as new as when Brian sent them as a birthday gift years ago. How his little brother would laugh at Leo's sweat and heavy breathing. Even the dog was moving easily, obviously slowing down to stay with him.

"Your four-wheel drive has me beat, girl."

She seemed to grin up at him, ears perked up, before she went back to watching the squirrels or whatever they were. Leo laughed and shook his head.

A bit labored or not, his breathing felt smooth and easy for the first time in longer than he could remember. The sharp evergreens mixed with the fertile earth to clear his head, and somehow his mind.

Ana was right. Leo didn't yet know the size or shape of it, but life would go on. *He* would go on whether he wanted to or not.

A couple of hours later, when the gnawing in his belly overcame the burning in his legs, he spotted a broad, flat rock near the stream. More than enough room for him and the dog to relax in the sun and enjoy whatever delicacies Costel had sent along. Leo sat with a groan, leaning forward to stretch his back and legs. He pulled the boots and socks off, sinking his toes into the damp moss a few inches away from the water. The soft, cool massage was heavenly on the burning soles of his feet.

True to his word, the innkeeper had packed a feast that looked like it would feed at least four people. Two huge sandwiches, two vacuum flasks full of hot tomato soup, several small red apples, and a bundle of some sort of meat jerky.

"I think this is for you," he said, handing a piece to the dog. She made short work of it and waited for more. "Don't worry, there's more than enough here to share."

Before he realized it, Leo had finished everything but a piece of the bread the dog was happy to help with. The cliché about being outdoors building up an appetite seemed accurate, at least out in these woods. He stretched out across the warm rock, enjoying the soreness of unaccustomed motion in his legs and lower back. The dog curled up on a pile of leaves not far away with a sigh.

Leo didn't plan to fall asleep, but he had no idea how much time passed before he woke. He sat up, shaking his head. He'd been out hard. Nothing should have gotten him out of a state like that, certainly not out here with his belly full and his body warm. Maria often complained about him sleeping like a log when he took a nap.

He noticed the silence then, the lack of any noise besides his own breath and the creek behind him.

The dog was awake too, sitting right beside him and staring

straight ahead. Leo reached down to pet her and felt a curious rumble in her chest. She was growling, low and soft.

"Something out there?" he whispered.

He thought he'd heard about bears up here, and maybe wolves, but he couldn't quite remember. His sleep-fogged brain was slow to get moving. The hair on his arms stood when the dog's growling deepened.

Were there mountain lions out here too? *That* he understood from living in California. He had no desire to run across one.

He didn't have a clue what to do about it.

The dog got up into a crouch, her head and ears shifting around constantly. She turned in a slow circle, the rumbling continuous.

Leo groped for his socks. He should at least get ready to run. Even if whatever it was caught up with him, he'd give it his best shot.

He still couldn't see or hear anything besides the dog and the water. The birds and other creatures seemed to have vanished.

"Which way is it?"

If the dog would just settle on one direction, they could head off in the other. Leo was afraid they'd walk right into whatever it was. She kept moving, staring in one direction, then shifting to another.

He finally got his boots laced and stood, managing not to groan this time. He picked up the pack, hoping his stiff legs would respond if he had to run.

But something was different.

Despite the dog's unrest and the unnatural silence, now that he was awake Leo was feeling calmer. Nothing bad was going to happen to him out here.

There was no reason to think that, not so far away from any houses with no one else around. He'd gotten the feeling that morning that no one down in the village besides Costel and Ana would care if something did tear him to shreds.

And still, Leo knew he was safe, as sure as he knew his own name.

"Come on, girl," he said, scratching between her ears. "We're fine. Everything's going to be fine."

She looked up at him, her cloudy eyes wide, nostrils flaring as she sniffed in one direction after another. She whipped her head around at a rustle on the other side of the stream. Leo saw a squirrel run halfway up a tree before it turned to watch them.

"See? Things are moving around again. It's all good."

The mama dog started panting instead of growling, and her tense legs and back relaxed a little. Leo knelt beside her, wincing when his knees crackled. They didn't hurt at all despite the noise. He just hated to see the dog jump because of him.

"Whatever it was has moved on. Either that or it decided it likes us too much to eat us. Ready to head back?"

She glanced around one last time, then looked into Leo's eyes. She drew a deep breath and sighed as plainly as any human could before she turned toward the village.

A few birds twittered, echoing each other on either side of the little valley. By the time Leo and his companion got back to the trail, their songs were nearly as loud as before.

The silence descended several more times on the much easier walk back down the mountain, but Leo never got the same uneasy sensation. The dog stopped for a few seconds each time, growling with her hackles raised all along her back. She let him comfort her, though he was sure she thought he was a fool for not getting upset.

Even after he walked back through the gate to Costel's inn, the sun setting behind him, Leo wondered whether he or the dog had been right.

Chapter 28

The satisfaction was deep. The renewal was strong.

Even after so much searching, so many decades of need, she'd never imagined the substance and joy she could draw from the life of another. As long as that other was the one she needed most.

For the first time, she was fulfilled by drinking, not drained. Invigorated, not tranquilized. She drank until the body had nothing left to give her. Nothing but the filthy blood that she didn't need.

Not yet.

So close, almost what she needed for the true recovery. There was more all around her, waiting for her to take it. And another she'd longed to destroy was near. One who'd worked to destroy her.

The taste was almost as sweet.

And still it was not enough.

The thinnest layer of ice, the slightest mist, kept her from her true form. Her whole form for the first time since she was barely old enough to walk.

She didn't need another soul to destroy, but one to love. One to cherish, one to hold dear for the rest of her long, long life.

She found him, and she went to him. And she gained recovery at last.

Chapter 29

THE DREAM STARTED as so many others had since she died. The dream that always turned into Leo's worst nightmare. Maria was naked, so warm and soft and sweet against him. Leo knew it was a dream as he took her into his arms. Even in his sleep, he always mourned her.

They fell into the familiar pattern, the habits of decades together, his body anxious to join with hers. Making love to Maria had always been easy, from the first time they touched. That didn't change even in her darkest times and deepest addiction. Not until she was so sick and weak that he was afraid to touch her at all.

Maria moved on top of him as she often did, the favorite way for both of them. She was light and ethereal, barely there, hardly enough to touch or even feel against his skin. Still he responded, his whole body straining toward her. Maria groaned and moved with him, reaching down and gripping his shoulders.

The pressure increased, growing slowly until Maria was no longer like a breath of air across his flesh. Leo felt the echo of her weight pressing against him, pushing him down into the hard mattress.

He grabbed her hips, shifting her a tiny bit. He cried out loud as the whispery warm air across his cock turned into the firm, moist, high intensity grip of his lover. Maria leaned forward and ground against him. He bent his knees and raised his hips underneath her, moving more quickly. She dug into the back of his shoulders, her fingers sinking into the muscles.

Maria opened her eyes. The squeeze on his shoulders deepened into pain, but Leo didn't care. The same squeeze, rhythmic and growing stronger, started up within her. Leo watched as Maria's mouth dropped open, and she never looked away from him.

Her body grew more substantial around him, moving out from that heat and grip and release. She rode the wave of her orgasm, groaning low in her throat. Leo had no choice but to go with her, moving her against him, squeezing her hips and thrusting until he joined her in ecstasy.

Before he was ready, Maria moved away and got to her feet, standing beside the bed watching him. In the light of dawn coming through the open window, Leo wondered in his dazed and sluggish mind if this were somehow real, her way of saying goodbye before he left this place forever.

Maria stepped closer to him, and he reached up and touched her belly. Her pale, smooth, unscarred belly. All the marks of her childhood surgery and all the attempts to repair the damage done were missing in this half-dream. Even her forehead was smooth and pale, the pitted dark scar missing. She leaned down and brushed the shaggy hair away from his face.

"Thank you, my love," Maria whispered, taking his hand.

Before Leo could respond, she was gone.

He drew in a deep breath and stretched. Echoes of pleasure still moved through his body. His raging and confusing wet dreams as a teenager had never come close to this. She'd felt utterly real at the end. He could smell her in the room, half of the sweet aroma they made together.

Leo hoped he would somehow still be able to catch that scent when he finally woke.

Chapter 30

THE FIRST ROOSTER of the morning startled Leo, jerking him into awareness. He grunted as he sat up, dream fog still clouding his senses. The odd soreness in his hips and back was strange and unexpected. Even his shoulders hurt. He stood under the hot water in the tiny open shower, not much more than an overgrown sink with a hand spray, hoping the muscles would loosen up.

Probably the long hike with a backpack yesterday, carrying food for himself and the old mama dog. He'd be back to his LA routines of aches and pains from sitting in too many meetings and way too damned much traffic, followed by the gym and endless massages soon enough.

He pulled on the door twice before he realized he'd locked the door instead of unlocking it, turning the knob the wrong way without thinking. That had to be the first time he had ever left it unlocked overnight here. Maybe he was ready to get back to his real life and routines, lonely as that life would be.

Low voices stopped Leo before he got to the stairs. No one else had been getting up for breakfast, much less even earlier for coffee. He caught himself hoping no one else had arrived before he realized how selfish that was. Much as he appreciated Costel and his family for taking such good care of him, Leo held no illusions that he was on a private retreat.

Life did go on, at least outside of his lonely little room and his lonely little mind.

He stopped halfway down, this time with his mouth hanging open, when he saw Ana sitting with the innkeeper. She was dressed, but Leo didn't think she'd combed her hair. Her eyes were red and swollen, and she clutched a handful of tissues. Costel sat with his blond head down, turning Leo's unease up a notch higher. When Ana saw him, she started crying and stood.

"Leo, Leo," she said, meeting him in a hug at the bottom of the stairs. "I'm so sorry. It's too much."

"Shah, what's too much?" he said, watching Costel for clues but not getting any help. "What's going on?"

Ana only cried harder, and Costel got slowly to his feet.

"It's Elena," he said, still not meeting Leo's eyes. "She's gone. She passed away."

The floor seemed to drop away from Leo's feet. He grabbed one of the high-backed wooden chairs to keep from falling with Ana's weight.

"I don't understand," Leo whispered. "What happened?"

"I'm not the one to tell you," Costel said, finally looking at Leo. "You need to speak with Igor. I will take you if Ana cannot."

"Wait, slow down," Leo said, stepping back from Ana. "Just tell me what happened. Ana?"

"I will take you, Leo," she said, trying to catch her breath. "She died overnight, at her sister's house. I can't say more, but I will take you to Igor."

"I'm not going anywhere until one of you starts making sense!"

Leo regretted his shout a second too late to stop himself. Ana was shaking her head and crying again, twisting a guilty knife into his heart. Costel pulled out a chair.

"I am sorry, my friend, but we cannot. Let me bring you coffee and food if you want. But it is Igor's place to talk to you."

Leo sat, mainly because his legs weren't willing to hold him any longer. He kept hearing the whispers of the villagers yesterday morning, seeing the old women crossing themselves when he walked by. The lovely walk in the woods beyond the inn with the ancient dog had given his mind a break, but he couldn't pretend their suspicious response to him had never happened.

And he couldn't pretend the almost painfully intense dream this morning hadn't happened either. The two didn't go together, not logically, but his mind didn't seem to care about that.

"Is this because of whatever happened yesterday?" he said. He took the coffee, his hands trembling enough to make the white cup clatter against the saucer. "Whatever everyone was so upset about?"

Costel put the customary plate of day-old pastry on the table, and he and Ana sat. No one touched anything but the coffee.

"Please, my friend," Costel said. "Promise to listen to Igor. I have no wish to hurt you, but troubles like this are his place."

Leo drank his coffee, watching the other two. Neither of them showed any signs of giving in, and he didn't want to upset them any more than they already were.

"I don't trust that guy," he said. "Igor. I'll talk to him if it will help you two, but I don't have to like it."

"No one likes any of this," Ana said, stirring her own coffee. "It's out of our hands now."

"Then talk," Leo said. "One of you, please. Tell me whatever you can. Don't make me go in there without a clue what I'm facing. I've had enough of that over the past two years."

"I told you as much as I could yesterday," Costel said. "This changes everything, and I can say no more. I am sorry."

Anger twisted up from Leo's gut to his head, the strongest anger he'd felt in months. The only anger he'd felt at someone besides Maria in longer than that.

He got to his feet. "Great. An old woman dies and everyone wants to take it out on the foreigner. Whatever works, huh? Just take me over there."

Shame tried to overtake the anger as the innkeeper and Ana both bowed their heads, but Leo refused to give it any hold. He'd known both of these people for more than half his life, and they were sending him off to some stranger over a damned superstition. Anger was the only thing that could possibly get him through such an absurd situation.

"I'll take you now," Ana said, wiping more tears from her cheeks. "I'm sorry too, Leo."

"Let's get this over with."

Chapter 31

Leo managed to keep quiet until he was in Ana's cramped sedan. She drove for several minutes without saying a word, heading through the village shrouded in heavy, thick fog. When she touched his arm but kept her silence, he'd had enough.

"What kind of mess are you dragging me into, Ana?"

"There's nothing I can do," she said, putting her hand back on the wheel. "I'm sorry."

"That's all anyone can say to me lately," Leo said, not caring that his anger was deepening into fury. "'I'm sorry.' If you ever cared about me, or about Maria, tell me what the hell is going on!"

"That's not fair," Ana whispered.

She didn't stop driving. Leo had never seen this part of the village before. Like so many in Transylvania, the neighborhood was filled with traditional white plastered houses with brown timber supports and reddish tile roofs. None were grand or huge, but all were neat and well-maintained.

"Tell me how it's fair for you to take me to this guy I've never even spoken to before, and I don't even understand what I've done wrong."

Ana parked in the freshly paved driveway of the largest two-story house Leo could see. The yard was filled with chickens and a garden, like so many others, and a steep wooded hillside lay behind it. A brand new metal roof made to look like the usual tile stood out as a sign of wealth, status, or both.

"You're right," she said, taking Leo's hand. Hers was terribly cold. "You haven't done anything wrong. This is what I know. Elena died early this morning, or at least that's when her sister found her. She had no blood on the sheets, no bruises. Nothing wrong they could see. She was holding her rosary, squeezing so tight it cut into her hand. The blood seemed frozen solid around the wound."

"Okay." Leo was glad he hadn't eaten. "That's awful. But how does that point to Maria?"

"They said...they said her eyes were wide open, and she looked like she was screaming. All the pictures of Maria, the ones her sister had from when she was a baby, your wedding photos, even a locket around Elena's neck. The glass on every one was broken."

"And that's why they think it was my wife?" Leo said, ignoring the freezing goose bumps racing over his flesh. "My dead wife? Because some glass was broken?"

The front door opened, and Igor stood watching them with his arms crossed. He was dressed for a day at the office, with pressed khaki pants and a dark blue polo shirt.

"I still live here, Leo." Ana kissed his cheek and let go of his hand. "I can't say more. Just know Igor was the head of the Communist Party here, but he was never one of them. He worked very hard to protect us. He still does."

Leo wanted to shout at her, to demand to know what that could possibly have to do with him, but she was already afraid. And she was making no move to get out of the car. He was on his own. She confirmed his suspicion by backing away and driving off as soon as he closed his door.

Igor watched Ana's tiny blue sedan. He didn't look back until Leo stepped right in front of him. Leo could absolutely imagine him in the role of Communist Party boss, right out of central casting. His thick black hair was barely longer than a crew cut, the part razor sharp. His moustache stiff and perfectly trimmed. Hair dye or not, he had to be at least sixty, but he showed no signs of age beyond several sharp lines across his forehead and around his mouth and brown eyes.

No matter who Igor was or who'd he'd been under a dead regime, Leo decided not to be intimidated as the silence stretched on. This man couldn't possibly hold a candle to insecure actors, demanding directors, or jumpy studio execs. Or to burying his wife barely forty-eight hours ago.

"Want to tell me why I'm here, Igor?" Leo said. "Sorry to be so familiar. Your last name is one of the many things I don't know."

"Igor will do," he said without moving. "I have the answers no one wants to hear."

"I'm quite sure I can take it. Start talking."

"I will remind you of that later," Igor said, pulling the door closed. "Walk with me, Leo."

He set off down the driveway, one of the few paved ones Leo had seen in the village. For whatever reason, this man had everyone else running scared. With Ana out of sight, Leo couldn't think of anything else to do but follow.

"Ana tells me Elena died last night," Leo said.

"She's dead, yes. Did Ana tell you what happened?"

"Only that Elena didn't seem to be hurt," Leo said. "She just died."

"Tell me if you still think that's so." Igor held out a large smartphone.

Leo took it without thinking and flinched when he saw the photo. Elena didn't simply look like she was screaming. Her mouth was drawn back, her face twisted and distorted, frozen in what had to have been a horrible shriek. Her eyes had the odd, flat look of death, reminding him forcefully of seeing the same look in his wife's eyes, but the fear hadn't left them.

"Not a mark on her, you see," Igor said. "Keep going."

Leo took a deep breath before he flipped to the next image. His mother-in-law's hand, fingers twisted into a claw, with her ancient wooden rosary gripped within. The long edge of the crucifix was digging into the flesh under her thumb, ripping the skin. The wound was deep and jagged, but none of the pooled blood welled out of the gash. Ana was right.

"Why are you showing me this?"

"Because no one has seen something like this in many years," Igor said, taking his phone back. "I'm not the only one who knows it must stop, but I am the one who must make sure it does."

Chapter 32

"Fair enough, Igor," Leo said. He matched the older man's fast pace along the deserted street. "I'll play along. I see a woman who wasn't young and who'd had a terrible shock when her only child died. She died herself, maybe a heart attack, maybe after a bad dream or something. That's what I see. What's your version?"

"When Elena was your age," Igor said, "Maybe a little younger, times were difficult here. All of Romania suffered, as did other Soviet Bloc countries. The trouble was worse in the mountains. Many starved and died, same as everywhere, but we were unable to keep up with the dead. The burials were too fast. A problem we thought dealt with long ago returned to us, and many more died because of that."

Leo closed his eyes and shook his head, trying to keep his temper in check. He couldn't imagine this was a reasonable time to play a practical joke, try to make the outsider look like an idiot. Everything else he could think of made even less sense.

"You're not going to tell me Dracula was real after all," Leo said. "Please tell me that's not it."

"No, nothing so crude and fanciful." Igor smiled, and Leo clenched his fists with the need to let his anger jump in and take over. "And nothing so easily solved. I've grown quite fond of Mr. Stoker's creation over the years. Brings in tourists and their money while deflecting from the truth at the same time."

"And what truth is that?" Leo said. "Zombies, rising from the grave to roam the countryside and stalk their grieving parents? Not the most original pile of horseshit I've heard, Igor."

"Another fiction from your American movies, one that would be easier to manage." He handed the phone to Leo again. "More of the grieving."

This time Leo flipped through several color images, then many more black and white. All showed faces remarkably like Elena's, the same terror resting uneasily alongside dead eyes. The quality deteriorated until he thought he was looking at a scan of an old tintype, but the fear was unmistakable.

"Just tell me," Leo said, giving the phone back. "I'm not in the mood for guessing games, or whatever kind of game this is."

They were walking in what seemed like circles, along narrow roads, passing tiny houses one after the other. The few people who were outside crossed themselves and went back in, just like the day before.

"We had our problem under control when I was very young," Igor said. "We thought it well on the way to elimination when the order came down from Ceaușescu. All families, all women, were to have as many babies as they possibly could. Large families were rewarded at a time when many were starving, and birth control or termination was illegal. This much you know."

"Yes. Elena suffered because she only had one," Leo said, fresh shock at her death twisting through his gut. "And she made choices she never should have for Maria."

"Now we come to the part you do *not* know," Igor said. "Elena and many others in our village made the only choices we could have. To keep a threat the Communists were never aware of and could not have understood from growing out of control."

Leo turned his head to hide his scowl and realized where they were. The steeple of the church where Maria now rested showed above a row of shops just to his left. At least he knew how to get back to the inn from here. From there to Bucharest and on to somewhere else, anywhere where the world still made sense.

Before he could speak, Igor held the phone out again.

"What is it this time?" Leo said. "Rows of peasants on stakes to intimidate outsiders?"

"I'm afraid Vlad's methods would not help us," Igor said. "This is what we've watched for for many centuries, and we must again today."

Images of fresh graves flipped by, starting in color and again shifting to black and white. They weren't sunken as so often happened before grass was replanted. These were rectangular volcanoes, the centers pushed up and driving cracks through the dry earth all around. No hokey claw marks like in the low-budget horror movies Leo and Brian had loved as kids.

In the middle of about half the graves, a perfectly round hole sat at the highest point. Once he got to the primitive images at the end of the album, Leo handed the phone back.

"If we see this, Leo, we must be prepared to take terrible action. We will also have no choice. Under Ceaușescu, as the number of births increased, the number of deaths did as well. We were not able to bury the dead properly, as we attempted to with your wife. What Elena did, and what I did with myself and my own children, was the only way we could defy the Communists and bring a terrible curse to an end."

They turned the corner of a high stone wall and stood at the back of the cemetery. Leo's eyes found Maria's grave despite his mind's orders to look away. The space was covered with piles of flowers that had been inside the church, ropes of garlic around and through all the rest. He breathed out through his chilled lips.

"I may not have any kind of legal standing here," Leo said. "But I'll do whatever it takes to keep you from digging her up, Igor."

"Even if she was not properly laid to rest, that will not be necessary," Igor said. He opened a huge black lock and swung the gate outward. "It would be far too late for that."

Leo followed on numb legs, his mind and his mouth filled with the pălincă he and Brian had finished the night before. Pălincă stolen from Maria's coffin and replaced with water.

A shadowy, moist corner of his mind, one that never encountered science or logic or even the plain light of day, wailed in terror at what he'd done. At what he was starting to believe he'd done in his waking dream that morning. If that part of him gained even a shred of control, Leo knew he'd either run screaming or curl up whimpering on the ground.

Igor stopped beside Maria's grave, beside his wife's final resting place, watching Leo walk toward him. When he squatted, Leo tried to join him. He landed hard on his knees instead. He managed to lean forward when the older man did and helped brush the flowers and braids of garlic away.

Chapter 33

The men's voices were faint from her hiding place, but Maria's hearing was as sharp and clear as ever. She stood in the smallest room in the back of the ancient building, supposedly the most sacred place in any Orthodox church. In contrast to the bright paintings and icons covering every surface in the nave, this room was plain white and undecorated. And while the nave itself was barely the size of an entryway in a typical American church, this space was hardly large enough to be a broom closet.

Maria adjusted the black skirt and white shirt yet again, stolen from a nearby clothesline, trying to get the too-large garments to hang comfortably. She glanced at the priest's holy robes and vestments, smiling at the thought of stealing those instead. She could stride through the village in embroidered golden garments taken from a room she was considered too unclean to step into as a living woman. The heavy cloth was cool and sensual under her fingers, increasing her perverse thrill at entering this forbidden space at last. Only the certainty she'd be caught kept her from taking the clothing.

Her heart, her strangely strong and beating heart, was breaking over the confusion and fear in her husband's voice. Igor kept on, using every prosecuting attorney trick in the book. Pushing Leo right up to the edge of the truth. Pulling back. Forcing Leo to take the next step himself. Showing him what had to be the same photos Paul and then she had dug up of graves and too many dead bodies to count. Building up the dread and suspense until her lover's mind had to be breaking under the strain.

She'd done every bit of that herself and more countless times in a courtroom, but she'd never considered what she was putting the person on the other side through.

Much as Maria wanted to dart outside and bring both Igor and the cruel cross-examination to an end, she wasn't strong enough yet. Her body was gaining power here despite Magda's warnings about churches being unsafe. Perhaps that was her atheist nature protecting her, or perhaps the whole sacred ground thing had been wishful thinking from generations afraid of the strigoi.

Afraid of her.

The voices moved away from the window, and Maria walked back out into the sanctuary. She found the same clear spot in the paintings on the windows that she and Ana had helped enlarge, a few scratches at a time, decades ago.

Igor squatted beside her grave, and Leo fell to his knees on the other side. His lovely long brown hair fell over his face, and she wished he hadn't pushed it back. Maria wiped a tear away at the horrible, lost look in his eyes as they cleared off the flowers and braids of garlic, exposing the hole where she'd escaped. Her grave looked exactly like those photos she'd obsessed over before she quite believed any of this was possible.

Before she'd died in Leo's arms.

The escape from her underground prison felt much like buildup and release she'd found in those same arms. Pressure and heat and movement toward life, churning and seething until Maria had no choice, no chance of resistance or control.

Her husband had given her the gift of a new body. She didn't need the one that would soon be trapped under the ground. Maria had no doubt Igor would know at least as much as poor Magda had, so she had to keep moving.

As long as she moved faster than Igor, she would keep herself alive and gaining strength. Until she could catch Leo alone and help him understand they could get away from here and be together, strong and healthy again.

Magda told Maria if the strigoi survived long enough, three short years, they were even able to have children. The children so cruelly denied Maria when she was one herself.

After the two men walked away, Maria stepped outside the church. The foggy village was unnaturally silent. No doubt she was the cause of that, and she would take full advantage. She'd heard enough to know Igor was taking Leo to the old woman's house, the last place she'd been before returning to her husband's bed.

She had none of the fantasy changes, no superhuman strength or ability to fly, but Maria was able to move silently. She'd never managed that trick in her first life. As long as she used her mind, the best weapon and defense she'd ever had, she'd stay one step ahead of Igor.

And she'd make damned sure to end him and whoever was foolish enough to join his little hunting party.

Chapter 34

THE RAISED and cracked soil of his wife's grave was as perfect as any special effects prop Leo had ever seen, as if a gifted artist had copied Igor's photos down to the last detail. And in the center, in the highest point, where Maria's silent heart should be resting six feet under the dirt, was a perfectly round, pitch black hole no bigger than a quarter.

"What does..." Leo said, stopping to force air into his frozen lungs. "What is this?"

"Was she buried properly, Leo?" Igor stood, brushed off his pants, and held out his hand.

Leo let him pull him up and sat heavily on uneven concrete steps a few feet away.

"You saw the coffin as clearly as I did," Leo said.

His ears rang in time with his pounding heart even as his mind struggled to find some kind of explanation. Any explanation besides the promise he'd broken, the promise made to a dying woman.

"I saw her," Igor said. "And you insisted on having time alone with her right before we brought her out here."

A dark shape moved to Leo's right, and he barely managed to bite back his scream. The ancient mama dog walked toward them, her ears and tail low. Leo held a shaking hand out to her, and she let him scratch her head for a few seconds before she lay down at his feet.

"What do you know of the dogs in our village?" Igor said, sitting down beside Leo.

The older man let the dog sniff his hand before he rubbed her back. Leo wasn't sure if Igor was trying to distract him or get him ready for some new kind of shock. He still wasn't sure what the first shock was going to mean to him.

"I don't know much," he said. "They're usually in pretty good shape even if they're strays. This old girl has been hanging around for a few days, especially yesterday. She walked up in the woods with me. When no one else would."

"You must not blame people for being afraid," Igor said. "Even the ones who aren't old enough to remember know the signs of trouble. We pass the most vital warnings along to our children, much like this dog has."

Leo forced himself to focus on Igor's words. Something about that felt important to him. And talking about anything besides his wife wandering the forest like some kind of zombie would be an improvement.

"I saw a bunch of her puppies," he said. "At least I think they were hers. They looked just like her. Yesterday morning. They all ganged up and made a stray run off. She didn't seem as healthy as these do."

Igor looked sharply at Leo. For the first time, he thought the older man was rattled.

"They forced a stray to run off?" Igor said. "Several other dogs did?"

"Yeah, this one, what looked like a bunch of her pups, and other dogs from the village. The stray ran off toward the woods and they calmed down. Barked like crazy, though."

"This was a mistake from the beginning," Igor said, almost to himself. "But we had no choice but to bring her back here. Tell me, have you noticed the photos here, in the graveyard?"

"Photos?" Igor had to be purposely keeping him off balance, but he had no hope of catching up at this point. Most of the old graves had small black and white photos under glass, beautiful and eerie at the same time. "You mean on the tombstones?"

"Older cemeteries all over Romania have them now," Igor said. "I understand other places in the world as well. At least in this village, they're not for sentimental value."

He held out the phone, and Leo considered refusing to look. He even considered taking it, smashing it against the steps, and walking away. But he knew it was too late for that.

The photos were in pairs, but not by married couples like the tombstone photos so often were. First the glassed-over tombstone image, then a photo of the real person. They didn't quite look the same, even though they were clearly the same person. The second image showed a healthier, maybe younger version. Leo's curiosity struggled through his fear and confusion.

"When were these second ones taken?"

"The photos are on the graves so people will remember what the deceased look like," Igor said, waving his hand out at the graveyard. "They must be recognized, no matter how long since they passed away."

"Must be...recognized?"

"The second photos are after death, Leo. The second death."

Leo was again certain Igor was playing some kind of horrible joke, with the worst kind of timing after he'd buried his wife and would have to be there for his mother-in-law. If anyone in the village would let him attend, of course.

"Listen, you've got my attention," Leo said. "I don't understand why, but you're scaring the hell out of me. They had to embalm Maria for the flight. If you're trying to tell me she's coming back, she won't get far."

"They do not come back sick or injured," Igor said, shaking his head. "They come back whole, as they were before death. If they were not whole, they could not have children once enough time has passed."

"Okay, that's enough," Leo said, getting to his feet. His wife's pale, perfectly smooth belly took up his entire mind. The dog shifted, but she didn't move. She just watched him. "I know I'm a foreigner here, but I'm not hanging around to be some kind of joke to you. Your idea of humor escapes me."

"Nothing is funny about this," Igor said. "We have prevented anyone from returning since the days of Communism, and we've done all we could to make sure Maria's generation would be the end of this curse. I've fought this my entire life, Leo. I'm more exhausted than you can possibly imagine. But I will not allow another line of strigoi to be born."

Chapter 35

The phone buzzed in Leo's hand, and he somehow managed not to drop it onto the stones. He gave it to Igor without looking at the number. The other man answered in Romanian, then held up his hand. Leo took one step, meaning to head back to the inn and get ready to leave.

His feet refused to move further, along with his lungs and his heart.

Such a harsh, uncomfortable word. *Strigoi.* The way it grated through his ears and into his mind. But Igor had said he would not allow another line to be born. Right after he said their bodies were perfect, so they could have children.

No part of him could deny Maria had been obsessed with that very thing.

What had he made love to that morning? Leo couldn't pretend he'd been dreaming any longer. His groin ached with strong contractions, far more than any dream could bring. Would he or anyone else be able to live with the consequences of whatever he'd done?

Igor's face paled, and he held his now trembling hand over his eyes. He spoke quietly for a few seconds before ending the call.

"The woman I wanted you to talk to," Igor said. "One of those who guided us, helped us try to put a stop to all of this. She is dead."

"If she guided you forty years ago," Leo whispered. "She has to be older than Elena."

"Certainly, she was," Igor said, his eyes narrow and his voice sharp. "She was in good health. And she was found in exactly the same state as Elena. Age has nothing to do with this."

"What are you saying it is, then?" Leo said. "Was she related to Maria, too?"

"No, not related. Was she buried properly, Leo? Whatever is done is done, but I must know what we face."

Leo tried to force air deep into his lungs, hoping that would slow his heart at least a little. He looked into the dog's eyes, dark brown and somehow wiser than most humans. He stared at the perfect, pitch black hole in his wife's grave.

"I didn't want her to be buried with alcohol," he said. His voice was quiet but surprisingly steady now that he was admitting to what he'd done. "Drinking is what killed her. I switched it out with water."

Igor was silent for several seconds. He glanced at his phone when it buzzed, then held it out to Leo. A woman who had to be at least ninety, hair thin and white, round face deeply lined, stared out at him. Her features were frozen in exactly the same expression of terror as Elena's and all the others had been.

"I respect your love for your wife," Igor said. "And your sorrow at losing her. I understand why you would not believe me. These two women did not have to die, not yet, and not in such a horrible way. If we do not stop her, this will happen to many others."

"Why these two?" Leo said, his mind searching for another explanation that his heart knew he wouldn't find. "I've never seen this woman or heard of her."

"When they return, they seek out the ones they knew in life," Igor said. "In the beginning, when they need to grow stronger, they often draw upon the human trait that can give us most terrible strength. Elena told me Maria deeply resented what we had to do. Is this true?"

"Yes. She hadn't spoken to her mother since she found out ten years ago. She spent those years and a small fortune trying to undo it."

"This dead woman gave us the good we needed to stop the evil,"

Igor said. "The magic of the old ways. Maria found the ones she hated most. And she will not stop there."

"What am I supposed to do about this?" Leo said. "Why tell me? You could have taken care of whatever has to be done here and let me go back to the US. Isn't it bad enough that I'll be going back alone?"

Igor stopped long enough to push the flowers back across the grave before he walked out of the graveyard and into the quiet street. Leo was again reduced to following with his brain unable to respond any other way. The dog did the same.

"She knows the ones she hates," the older man said. "Just as she knows the ones she loves. She will eventually find you whether you help us or not, and she will trust you. You can get close enough to her to bring this to an end without anyone else risking their lives."

Leo knew his face was pale, and Igor watched him too closely to have missed it. He'd already been close to Maria, closer than he ever thought he'd be to her or anyone else.

"If I refuse?" Leo said. "If I pack up and leave today? Are you saying she'll find me across the Atlantic?"

Leo glimpsed the Communist party boss as Igor stopped outside the gate. He stood tall, shoulders squared, lip curled upward just enough to show his contempt.

"Given enough time, I'm certain she'd find you in the end," Igor said. He sounded like he thought that was exactly what should happen. "Responsibility for the first *strigoi* in decades rests with you. With your stubborn refusal to respect our ways even though we took a great risk in allowing you to bring her here. The risk of leaving the ignorant people in America exposed to her was far worse. I would think you'd want to be husband enough, man enough, to take that responsibility instead of running away."

"You expect me to lure her somewhere and kill her again?"

"This is not your wife, Leo. Not the woman you loved. This is not even human, except in that a new line of cursed souls can spring from it. This is a monster that will murder me and everyone else in this village unless it is destroyed."

"If she's not in her grave, how the hell am I supposed to find her?" Leo said. He wasn't sure if he was about to scream or sob.

"I told you I wanted you to talk to the second woman who was murdered," Igor said. "You'll talk to her granddaughter now. She will know how to find her and what to do. This dog will guide you both. That is their role, and we're most fortunate she and her offspring remember."

Chapter 36

THE VILLAGE high up in the mountains, much higher than Costel's inn and Igor's party boss dominance, had been deserted for more than thirty years. Ana told Maria the truth years ago about people returning to maintain the houses, though. The small yards were still neat and clean with the recent attention, dirt roads patched and cleared of winter debris, rustic timber fences in good repair.

One house, low to the ground and painted white like all of the others close by, gave no sign of being occupied again. No smoke rose from the gray stone chimney. The doors and windows were closed and covered with white shutters. There was no electricity for lights, inside or out.

And yet a sort of life had returned to the seventh house on the main street. The life may have been unusual and unexpected, but the woman inside the house wasn't surprised in the least.

Maria stood naked in the sitting room of her maternal grandparents' house, where she and her mother were born. The ceiling was only a couple of inches above her head, and the entire room was smaller than her walk-in closet back in California.

The furniture she remembered from visits when she was young was almost all gone, hauled down from here in a horse-drawn wagon to her aunt's house when the village was abandoned eight years ago. A built-in sitting area with no cushions, the built-in shelves in the tiny kitchen, and a broken mirror in front of her were protected from thieves or curious hikers by faded blue curtains covering the tiny, low windows.

The mottled and crazed reflective surface was hardly ideal, and the light was dim. But Maria could see more than enough. She turned to the left and right, catching the best angle she could. Her body was healthy. Her body was whole.

For the first time in her memory, she ran her hands over a smooth and unscarred abdomen. Even the deep scar on her forehead, the sobriety reminder that failed her in the end, was smooth and flawless.

"Better than the best surgeon in Beverly Hills," she said under her breath.

Maria held no illusions, no confusion about where she was and how she got there. The booze had killed her at last, just like she'd always feared. Just like she'd wanted in the end.

Neither her dread nor Leo's had been enough to stop her once the disease took hold of her again, and her body had succumbed to the renewed abuse. Her memory of that time was hazy with illness and pain medication, but she knew.

Worse, she had a strong idea what she'd put Leo through.

Leo was here, though, and her husband had given her the last push she needed to create this perfect new body. None of her studying or conversations in the retirement village in Austria had quite explained how that worked, and it was one of the few things Maria didn't care to learn more about. It worked. She was living, breathing proof. In those moments of realization, of her new life exceeding her oldest dreams, all Maria cared about was being in a strong body with her stronger mind intact.

As surely as Maria knew she was breathing the musty air despite drawing her last in that antiseptic hospital room, she knew she couldn't stay here. Frail Magda Schmidt, her mind long since lost to her dementia, had warned Maria without meaning to. Staying in the ground she'd been buried in or the house she'd been born in would send her right back into a permanent death.

Maria caressed her belly again, her fingers straying lower into the thick, glossy hair and the exquisitely sensitive folds beneath. The nerves were as revitalized as the rest of her, crying out for more attention and release.

She shifted one foot onto the plaster seat, slipping one, two, three fingers as deeply inside as she could, creating pressure from within and without. Maria's breathing deepened, and her knees nearly buckled with her orgasm, stronger and faster than when she was a teenager.

Leo. She needed Leo.

Not only for the pleasure he'd been all too willing to provide that morning, though Maria needed that more than she had for years. And not only for the chance to make a baby with him at long last, to erase the meddling of her mother and that awful old woman.

She needed Leo's protection if she was to survive long enough to be able to leave this place. Long enough to give him the children he wanted so badly.

The thought of her mother took some of the pleasure and joy, and Maria got dressed in her stolen peasant clothing. Whatever her reasons or justifications, she was a murderer. She'd not only killed her own mother, but she'd killed a very old woman.

She left the house of her birth and walked in ever widening circles, taking one route, then another, into and out of the empty village. Anyone, or anything, tracking her, would be confused by the overlapping trails. Magda's praise of the dogs that helped with the *strigoi* had proven true when she'd followed Leo in the woods the day before. The grey-muzzled dog had known she was there, every single time.

Maria had no doubt she'd kill Igor and whoever he brought with him just as quickly and easily as she'd taken her vengeance upon the two old women. Once she was safe and away from here with Leo, she'd work out how she felt about all of that.

Until then, all that mattered was her own survival.

Chapter 37

THE OLD WOMAN'S house was not nearly so large or grand as Igor's. The one-story building sat at the end of the paved roads of the village, with only a dirt and gravel path twisting up into the woods beyond. When Leo, Igor, and the dog arrived, a young woman stood outside. Leo remembered her from the funeral, the quiet figure in a modest black dress talking with Elena.

Today she wore faded blue jeans and a black t-shirt gone nearly gray. She'd caught her long, brown hair in a rough ponytail, and Leo guessed she was in her early thirties. The cigarette in her hand made him wonder how far off he was, especially if she smoked as much as so many people in Romania. He'd learned over the years to simply be grateful the smoke wasn't nearly as foul as American brands.

"Igor," she said. "Thank you for coming so quickly."

"I am very sorry about your grandmother," Igor said, kissing both of her cheeks. "Sanda, this is Leo."

"Her time was short," Sanda said. "And she knew the risks she took. Elena's death pains me more deeply. You understand what's happening here, Leo?"

"I don't understand anything," Leo said. "I know my wife is gone, and Igor believes she had something to do with all of this. I'm sorry about your grandmother either way."

"All we can do now is make sure all the souls we've lost are at peace," Sanda said. She knelt, and the dog went right to her, wagging her tail furiously. "You've brought a powerful ally for our journey."

"Journey?" Leo said. "I don't know where I'd be going. Or why."

Sanda looked up at him, and the morning light caught her light blue eyes. Those eyes were daring him, sure, but her whole demeanor was shaming him more openly than Igor had. She'd go without him if she had to. And right now she expected to.

"All I have is a guess," she said. "This old girl will be our best guide. The dogs always have been."

"I know this makes me sound like the biggest coward in Europe," Leo said, "But assuming I believe any of this, why would you want me to go? I'm not some kind of hunter or tracker. I've never killed a damned thing in my life."

"I explained what has happened," Igor said, looking at Sanda. "Leo knows he is at least partially responsible, though I wonder if we ever should have let her come back here."

"We had no choice," Sanda said, standing beside the two men. She barely came up to Leo's shoulder, but he was more than intimidated by her attitude and confidence. "Burying her somewhere else would be a disaster. What part did you play in this, Leo? In her coming back?"

"I can't..." Leo stared up the path beyond the house, up into the woods he'd been so at peace in just yesterday, despite the odd silences. That seemed like a thousand years ago. "I know something's going on here. I'm not stupid. But I'm not having an easy time accepting my undead wife has anything to do with it. For the record, I switched the pălincă in her coffin for a bottle filled with water."

"Why would you do this?" Sanda said, crossing her arms.

"She drank herself to death. I couldn't stand the thought of her buried with what killed her."

Sanda shrugged. "And so that's what enabled her to come back instead. It is done now. All we can do is deal with the result. At least we know one of her weaknesses. We'll be ready."

"Let me know what I can do," Igor said. "When will you set out?"

"We leave as soon as Leo is ready," she said. "Once word of my grandmother's death gets around, you will not want to be in the village anyway. Terrible dreams for so many and two deaths the next day. This one gains strength far too quickly."

"This dog and her pups chased a stray away from the inn where Leo was staying yesterday morning," Igor said. "The strigoi was powerful before it even arrived here. I suspect Maria was already drawing strength on the flight from America. And I suspect Leo hasn't told me all he knows."

Leo closed his eyes, remembering Brian's restless flight, with everyone on board having bad dreams. Had that poor stray dog been the start of all this?

"Then we have no time to waste," Sanda said. "Igor, if you could bring pălincă, that would save us from having to go buy it. We'll meet you at the cemetery. I have everything else I need ready in the wagon."

Igor nodded and brought out his phone yet again. Sanda started toward the back of the small house, the dog at her heels.

"Have you decided I'm going along?" Leo said, hoping he wasn't loud enough to wake the neighbors. "I don't know where you're planning to take me or what you plan for me to do."

"Whether you go or not, I will be going to find this beast you've helped set loose," she said, walking slowly back, hands on her hips. "I will start in the village where Maria and so many other strigoi were born. My grandmother chose this house because the old road is here. They often return to where they were born when they're strong enough."

She stood inches away from him, the toes of her worn brown boots almost touching his nearly brand new ones.

"And you must understand one thing, Leo. If you interfere with me, I will not hesitate to do whatever it takes to stop you. This is not a game or a story to frighten the children. Not here. Not to me."

"Heed her words," Igor said, standing behind Leo with his arms crossed. "Such things have happened in the past. We will not let this cycle start again."

"Sanda, I don't mean to insult you," Leo said. "But if Igor is telling me the truth, you're too young for this. He said the last time this happened was before you could have been born. I know you're not older than me."

"No, I'm not older," she said. "But my grandmother and my father both trained me, and I know what I see. Two deaths are more than enough. You have ten minutes to decide what you will do. Either meet me back at the cemetery and listen to every word I say, or leave me to do my job."

Chapter 38

Leo stood in the driveway for several breaths, again unable to move or think. Sanda disappeared around back of the house. Igor was walking back the way they'd come. Even the dog had gone with her, leaving him utterly alone.

A vision of the old women's faces yesterday, dropping their eyes and crossing themselves compulsively as they walked away, sent him into motion. He couldn't stay out on the street, not if even half the people who lived here believed the stories. He walked unsteadily, then more quickly, after Igor.

"I need to get back to the inn," Leo said.

"Have you made your decision, then?" The older man didn't look at Leo or slow his pace.

"I don't have much choice, do I?" Leo said. "I at least have to get out of sight. From what you say and the way everyone's acting, someone will take me apart if I'm seen."

"I don't think we're as barbaric as all that," Igor said, glancing at Leo at last. "But no one would be happy to see you. From the inn, you're free to leave. Go back to Bucharest and the US if you will."

"I know," Leo said. "And I'm free to go with Sanda."

"You do hold responsibility for what has happened. And you are the one Maria will trust. She's already shown that, hasn't she?"

Leo took several steps before he answered.

"Yes," Leo said. "This morning. I didn't understand, any more than I did about the whiskey. I thought I was dreaming."

"No one warned you," Igor said. "At least not about the real reason for the whiskey or what else to watch for. We didn't realize she was so strong before she arrived. No one your age besides Sanda would know the true danger. For that, I am truly sorry."

"Why do we have to go back to the cemetery?" Leo said. His flesh crawled at the thought of digging up a corpse, no matter what state it was in. "You told me she wasn't there anymore."

Igor shook his head. "No, I did not. I told you digging her up would do us no good. There are other things we can do."

The roads and yards were more deserted than they'd been the day before. Leo didn't even see anyone looking out the windows. They were all terrified of him. Or terrified of whatever had visited him that morning. He stopped when Igor did at the driveway to the inn.

"Will I be wasting my time to wait for you, Leo? Or should I just call a car to take you to the airport?"

Leo looked up at the third floor balcony, the room where he'd shared so many wonderful days and nights with his wife. Until that morning, he'd thought they'd made love for the last time many weeks ago. Back when he never could have imagined what he was slipping into believing right now.

"Just let me get my things," he said. "I don't want to cause anyone else trouble over this."

Leo was relieved he didn't see Costel or anyone else on his way upstairs. He couldn't possibly stay here any longer, no matter what was really going on. If everyone had already decided he was at fault, Costel and his family might suffer for letting Leo stay on. That was too high a price for a comfortable night's sleep.

He shoved his clothes and toiletries into his suitcase. He grabbed his heavy raincoat out of the wardrobe last, the first time he'd touched it since the daze of packing in Los Angeles. When he sat on the edge of the bed to change into his hiking boots, a painfully familiar scent rose around him. Leo leaned closer to the rumpled sheets.

His hands shook when he laced up the boots. That was her.

Unmistakably Maria, and not the faint, somehow diminished aroma of when they'd last made love. This was his wife in her full, healthy, lustful glory, as strong as right after they'd met in college. That vibrant woman, lost two years ago to booze and age and illness, had been in his bed this morning.

Leo tried to stop. He already believed this insane thing, so there was no need to torment himself.

He stepped back into the tiny bathroom anyway, unbuttoning his shirt and slipping it halfway down his back. He turned and looked over his shoulder. Four distinct bruises, the size and shape of Maria's fingers, stood out against his skin. He stared until his neck muscles cramped, his breathing slow and regular. Distant excitement started up in his belly.

No dream. No grief-driven hallucination. His love had been here. He'd made love to her, and he'd let her walk away. Now his only chance to find her again was to go with a woman who was determined to kill her, to put her under the ground again.

This time forever.

Leo met his own gaze in the mirror, and the crazed glare frightened him more than the thoughts taking shape in his pounding head. His neck creaked when he finally looked down and buttoned his shirt.

"Pull it together, man," he whispered. "If that was her, she's a fucking vampire or something worse."

A soft knock nearly forced a scream out of Leo, the second time that had happened in less than an hour. Igor opened the door.

"It is time. No one will think less of you if you can't do this, Leo. I've brought about the second death more times than I care to count, but I don't believe I could end my own wife."

"Has anyone ever?" Leo said, rubbing at his shoulder, pressing his fingertips into the bruises. "With their spouse, I mean."

Igor crossed his arms and leaned against the door frame. The party boss had returned.

"Are you asking me if anyone has ever brought their spouse back on purpose? Or if they have brought them to the second death?"

"Either," Leo said, looking into Igor's brown eyes. "Both."

"The only way this can end well is for the thing that looks like your wife to die," Igor said. "Do you understand me? If you do not, I will have my son take you to Bucharest now and I will accompany Sanda. If you decide you're man enough to take the responsibility for this, I will stay here and do my best to calm everyone. I'll join you both as soon as I can."

A jolt of dismay nearly as deep as the sight of all of those empty gin bottles in the hidden pantry broke Leo out in a cold sweat.

No.

Whatever happened, or did not happen, this would begin and end with him. Not with a stranger. With these two determined to bring Maria's unbelievable second life to an end, he wouldn't have the chance to make his own decision. Or find out what Maria's choice would be.

He picked up his suitcase and closed the door behind him, leaving the carved wooden key holder in the lock for the last time.

"I understand what I'm responsible for, Igor. Let's go."

Chapter 39

SANDA PACED BACK and forth in front of the church when Leo and Igor returned, smoke rising from her cigarette to join the lingering mist. The village was still and deserted except for the three of them and the mama dog. A cardboard box sat on the church steps.

"What kept you?" Sanda said, watching Leo. "Will I be going alone after all?"

"I'm going," Leo said. He wished for a hit of what had to be pălincă to slow his raging thoughts. "Why are we here?"

"We must make sure she can never return to this body," Sanda said, jerking her chin toward the graves. "Or if she is forced to, that she will be unable to leave."

Igor opened the gate and picked up the box, and Leo followed Sanda into the cemetery. The dog sat on the grass just inside the fence.

"How could she come back to this body?" Leo said.

"If we do not properly trap her in the one she has now," Sanda said. "Which we will do."

Leo gritted his teeth to keep from asking more questions. He had no idea what he would be able to go through with or not, but for these two to suspect him would be the end of any choices he had left. Even if those choices were too insane to admit, even to himself.

Igor again knelt and cleared off Maria's grave. That volcanic surface and eerily perfect hole startled Leo nearly as much as it had the first time. Sanda held out the clear glass bottle.

"If you wish to do your part," she said, "this is where that starts."

Leo took the bottle, resisting the urge to drink as much of it as he could in one swallow.

"What am I supposed to do with this?"

"The reason for the alcohol in the casket is to keep the body in the grave," Igor said from behind Leo. "It will serve the same purpose now. If the strigoi returns to this place, it will be over."

"Then what's the garlic for?" Leo said, touching one of the braids with the toe of his boot.

"We don't do just one thing," Sanda said. "If she hadn't been so strong when she went into the ground, the garlic may have been enough."

Leo stepped forward. He saw Maria's eyes in the hospice ward, yellow and dull. He saw them still and lifeless. And he saw them soft and fierce with passion just a few hours before. He was afraid his mind would split into pieces if he saw her in the flesh again, but the last thing he wanted was for her to return to the middle of this village.

He poured the whole bottle of pălincă into the hole in the middle of his wife's grave.

"Is that it?" he said, looking at Igor and Sanda. "No foam or smoke or anything?"

"This is not a movie, Leo," Sanda said, her voice cold and angry. "If she returns to this body, she will be held there as she should have been from the beginning."

"And the rest?" Leo said, pointing toward the box. Seven more bottles were inside.

"That is for when we bury her again," Sanda said.

Chapter 40

The first time Maria had visited Transylvania again after years of correspondence, Ana had taken her to these odd little rooms on the mountainside. The bars like a prison cell set into the rock were loose enough for two seventeen-year-old girls to move, with thick wooden posts all around them rotted nearly to dust. They both knew they'd be forbidden from returning if they were ever found out. So they'd never asked the older generation, still reeling that summer from the collapse of the USSR just a few months before.

Their best guess was a cave, perhaps natural to begin with, expanded with some kind of tool that left gouges in the dark gray rock. Three chambers were on either side of the main one, each with what looked like chairs and beds hewn into the stone. A few animal bones in each one only deepened the mystery.

Serious questions by candlelight so long ago, still unanswered. Was this an ancient storeroom? A hiding place from some war? Or a prison for those who must be truly forgotten?

Maria didn't miss the perfection of hiding out here herself, nor of never bothering to ask an adult about this place once she became one. As far as either of them knew, she and Ana were the only ones who'd been here in decades.

And Leo. She had no idea who she could trust outside of those two. Quite likely no one.

She sat on the long bench or bed or whatever it was in the center chamber, thinking of when she'd brought Leo here. Their first overseas trip together, back when saving up for the flight had been a struggle. Long before they didn't have to think twice about the first class fare. She'd brought him here, feeling vaguely disloyal to Ana, and they'd made love on this same spot.

Her fully recovered libido hadn't lessened throughout the day. Just the thought of that long ago afternoon, the delightful contrast of the cold stone with Leo's hot mouth and the heat of his body, had her aching for him again. Maria couldn't get distracted, not with Igor on the hunt for her.

She had to deal with that threat before she could turn to her restored future with her husband and the family they'd make together. Magda thought the curse that kept Maria barren through so many efforts and even surrogacy wouldn't outlive the woman who'd anchored it into so many young bodies.

Magda hadn't been certain, though. There was no way to know until the woman died. Maria put that out of her mind, resolving to keep it there until she could do something about it. For now she had to get herself and Leo safely away.

Maria walked into each of the other chambers, the path full of leaves and dirt, falling back into her habit of pacing while she worked through a problem. Once they fouled her grave, they'd want to find any other place sacred and safe to her. Maria hoped Costel and his inn would never cross Igor's mind.

She'd be forever grateful to Costel and his family for sheltering her and Leo so many times, and for taking care of him over the past few days. They didn't deserve to be punished for the part they'd unknowingly played in her full return to her body that morning.

Next would have to be the village she'd just left, the place of her and her mother's birth. Igor would want to keep Elena from returning to the same sanctuary if they didn't manage to bury her properly. Maria stopped pacing, chewing her lip and staring out the bars she'd dragged back into place.

That may be the best place to eliminate Igor and his hunting party and remove the threat forever.

Magda had been willing to talk to Maria several times, and not only because of her advancing dementia. She and Igor and others like them had worked hard to make sure the younger generations wouldn't pass their curse along. Partly by mutilating their bodies and subjecting them to the old woman's horrible spells, but also by keeping the knowledge hidden.

Ana had only heard rumors and legends. Maria doubted anyone her age or younger would have known it was possible she could be standing here alive, much less how to prevent it.

She left the chamber, making sure the door and the path were once again hidden. Maria had no doubt she would succeed, but she knew taking on Igor and his aged companions would take a lot out of her in her still-fragile state. As she had throughout her life, she trusted that her mind would bring her though any challenge victorious.

After that, she'd turn to her heart. And to Leo.

Chapter 41

THE NARROW TRAIL through the woods was as lovely as Leo remembered. Moss grew up out of the streambed overflowing with snowmelt and rain, close to the shaded dirt path. The steep trail was higher than the one he'd hiked with the dog, so much so that the hardwoods were just starting to bud, flashes of red and pink scattered throughout the towering firs and pines. He winced, wondering if they'd pass by the stump of the one that stood beside Maria's casket for the funeral.

Leo's mind tried to draw away from the fresh reality, but his resistance grew weaker with every beat of his heart. The sacrificed tree would never bloom this spring even though his beloved lived again.

The wagon was far smaller than the ones he'd ridden in the back of, snuggled under a blanket with his wife and others from the village. Instead of two long seats stretching back from the driver's bench, there was only a small squared off wooden compartment, not much different from a pickup truck in the US. His sleek black suitcase was absurdly out of place with an axe, the box of alcohol, a can of what smelled like gasoline, and several bundles covered in faded brown canvas.

The massive, glossy horses pulling those huge wagons were replaced by a shorter, more slender version. Her rich chestnut legs and shoulders rippled with muscles, though, and she switched her long black tail as if to complain about the lack of effort they expected of her.

The mama dog slept curled up on the narrow bench between them, saving Leo from feeing uncomfortable or obligated to talk. He was already afraid Sanda would overhear his racing thoughts.

Maria was alive!

Breathing and out there somewhere, right this minute. She was alive, and Leo was on a trip with a woman determined to kill her again. He couldn't pretend these weren't the consequences of murders already committed, of his mother-in-law and Sanda's grandmother.

He also couldn't pretend he wasn't trying to figure out how to save his lover from another death, one she would not miraculously survive.

That made him a madman, certainly, and perhaps a monster in his own right. Especially if he had to help Maria find a way to sustain herself with unknown macabre nutrition. Leo's hold on his own sanity had been slipping bit by bit since he found the gin bottles hidden away in their house. He knew he was dangerously close to losing his last fragile grip.

He didn't yet care. He wouldn't care until he had his wife safe and away from here, whatever that turned out to mean.

"Be alert, Leo," Sanda said, startling him. "We're nearly to the old village."

The road, nearly reclaimed by the forest around it, took a sharp turn up and to the right. He remembered bits and pieces from his first trip up here with Maria. They'd been falling in love, and they'd hiked all morning to spend the night in the house she'd been born in. Fewer than ten people, each of them well into their sixties, had lived up here by then.

None of them had seen him set off in a different direction with his new wife the next morning. To Maria and Ana's secret place, one Leo hoped was still a secret.

"When did they abandon this place?" he said. "I remember Maria being upset about it."

"Eight years ago. My grandmother was the last to agree to leave. She wouldn't have unless everyone promised to return in the spring and autumn to keep the place cleaned up and repaired."

"Why?" Leo said. "Surely no one wants to live all the way up here again."

"I would," Sanda said, with the first smile he'd seen. "I loved visiting my grandmother. I stayed with her all summer and every other chance I got. She insisted on the repairs because she was old and she hated to see things change. And because she wanted us to keep an eye on the place."

"In case something like this happened," Leo said, staring at a small waterfall off to the left. "In case of someone like me."

"Not only like this, Leo. Elena wasn't the only one who carried this curse to leave Romania years ago. Many were born in this village. My grandmother hoped if we returned often enough, we'd notice signs of any strigoi sheltering here. Perhaps those buried somewhere else where the customs and warnings were not known, making their way back home at last."

Leo's throat was too dry to swallow.

"What do you watch for?" he said. "In the old village, I mean."

"I'm told most of the beasts were confused and upset in the beginning," Sanda said. "It rarely occurred to them to be careful, to avoid leaving evidence. Hardly anyone Maria's age would know enough to stay hidden."

He nodded and looked away again. He'd never met anyone who absorbed everything around her the way his wife did. He'd seen her reading books about Romanian folklore a few times before she got so sick, claiming it was so she could explain her heritage to their children. If anyone could figure out how to stay safe, it would be her.

He'd have to be on the alert and make sure Sanda was the ignorant one.

The gears in Leo's head slipped a little bit more.

Chapter 42

MARIA WALKED toward her mother's village. Despite her silent movement and joy in her new body, she wished she could still drift like the mist along the ground.

Something did not feel right here. Something dangerous.

The wagon's creaking wheels brought her to a stop far beyond the edge of her circling exit paths. The eerily perfect and empty houses were between her and the path back down the mountain. Maria crouched behind a sprawling oak tree, her view unobstructed and her position well-hidden.

After her early morning flight with nothing but the stolen clothes she wore, Maria knew she might have to observe at first. She needed more information. She had to know the strength and weakness of Igor and anyone he brought with him. If she had to, she'd wait until one or all of them slept.

She would use weapons if she found them, but she had no need once she was close enough. Time and regaining a body that was starting to crave a more substantial kind of fuel hadn't dulled her ability to draw the energy of another living being. One old man, or one old man's guard, would be easy enough to dispose of. Guns or knives or whatever else they had would never come into play. Not unless she took them and used them herself.

A small chestnut horse passed the last curve in the road a few hundred yards away. Maria's unease didn't leave her, but seeing only two people on the wagon boosted her confidence. Igor had underestimated her, and badly. That didn't even look like him sitting beside a small young woman. This was a much younger man.

A man far too familiar to her.

Leo.

The horse let out a high, piercing cry, jolting the wagon to a stop. Maria tried to control her gut-wrenching reaction, squeezing her eyes closed and gritting her teeth. If every creature in the forest startled, all running away from where she crouched, she would be painfully easy to catch and put to the second death.

"Why?" she whispered, covering her mouth.

The woman brought the wagon into the middle of the village, barely a hundred yards away now. Maria knew her from past visits—a grandchild of the old woman who'd cursed her body after corrupt doctors butchered it so long ago.

Her reeling mind brought the name forward with the same easy efficiency as ever. Sanda. Sitting proud and plain beside Maria's husband, without even the decency to sneak up here under cover of darkness.

Sanda climbed down off the wagon. She walked toward the house with a long blade in her hand. Leo didn't move. Was he there to be some kind of guard? To keep watch and make sure Sanda completed her task without incident?

Or was he there to try to protect Maria?

Leo finally moved, nearly falling when he climbed down. He turned back and picked something large off of the bench.

Maria drew farther back, her heart thudding in her chest. Her husband was holding the same old dog that had tried to warn him in the forest. Back before he'd given Maria her body and the second chance she'd so desperately wanted.

Now he traveled with the granddaughter of a woman Maria had murdered the night before, and he'd brought the creature most likely to track her down so they could kill her.

Had she misjudged her lover so badly? Had Igor's brutal questioning and seeing how she'd escaped from the grave driven him over the edge and out of her life forever?

The dog trotted into the house, nose low to the ground and ears high. Leo slowly followed. His weaving gait reminded Maria of watching a drunk walk, one who was convinced he'd fooled everyone. That made no sense, but he stopped and gripped the low white fence like he was within moments of passing out.

Nothing about this made sense.

He finally straightened and went into the house, only to come back out barely a minute later. He walked more steadily when he returned, but he stopped and held on to the fence again. Maria stepped closer before she could stop herself.

If she could catch him alone, even for a few seconds, she could figure out where his loyalties were. Or maybe she could change them back to her.

Leo moved then, walking back to the wagon. Maria strained to see what her husband was carrying toward the house to help the woman determined to kill her. A can that probably held gasoline, if they were sticking to Magda's playbook for strigoi destruction. And...pălincă.

She flinched, rubbing her jaw without realizing it. The reflex was nowhere near as strong as with gin, but her lips, her tongue, her throat could feel the burning, numbing liquid pouring down. The craving she'd fought her whole life started with that brandy, with her grandmother giving her a sip for a toothache before she even had the words to ask for help. One of Maria's earliest memories, and one of her strongest.

Despite her restored body, her mental weakness for alcohol had followed her beyond death. If anyone in the world could have known that was possible, it would be the man who held her when she took her last breath.

If Leo had brought booze up here, he had to be working with Sanda and Igor, not against them.

He walked back out with the dog on his heels. He poured the pălincă in a line around the edge of the house. She could think of no reason why he'd ever do that to help her.

Maria had a choice to make, one of the first in a long while. Her life hadn't been much worth living until she'd met Leo so many years ago. If he wouldn't protect her and help her survive long enough to leave this place, her prospects were as dim as they'd been back then. Drinking too much, wasting time drifting through college, not accepting for one second that anything about herself was worth a damn or any effort to improve.

He'd changed all that. By simply believing she was worth saving, worth caring for. Leo had pushed her to not only survive her own self-destruction, but to thrive and prosper. If he'd truly turned his back on her, she might be better off letting Sanda run her through with that blade, pin her to the ground so she'd never roam the earth again. Or walking into that house under her own power and letting the flames do the job instead.

She shook her head, wiping tears away. Besides the will and ability to live and actually enjoy her life, Leo had helped her discover another trait that served her well. As an attorney, Maria Sabov was either respected, feared, or hated for her iron will and rock-solid determination. She did not scare easily, and she gave up even less often.

When Leo walked to the back of the house, out of her sight, Maria stood and walked down out of the woods. She was a hundred feet from a small, narrow barn, the high roof thatched with thick grass. She hadn't helped in any of the cleanups since the village had been abandoned, but she had a good idea what would be kept in there.

Tools, supplies, equipment.

Weapons as good as or better than the blade Sanda carried.

Chapter 43

THE LAST TIME Leo visited the village where Maria was born, several people still lived there. Many of the children, grandchildren, and great-grandchildren had made the trip then. The narrow streets had been teeming with people. The change could not possibly have been more stark.

The only thing close to the strangeness, the dislocation from reality, was walking onto an empty movie or TV set. His staggering mind insisted everything was fake, that a stiff enough wind would make the facades of low, white houses shudder or even fall over. Any second now, people from special effects or set decoration would come around the corner with trees or boulders slung casually over their shoulders. The last bit of unreality needed to complete the perfect illusion.

Sanda set a brake on the wagon and climbed down, her eyes constantly moving. She pulled a long hand blade, a lot like the machetes Leo and Brian used without nearly enough supervision growing up in Ohio. She held it with the comfort and ease of long practice, low in front of her body.

That gleaming sharp blade, the torches and gasoline, the bottles of pălincă. Everything in the wagon, including Sanda and the dog waiting patiently for his help down from the high bench, were there for one purpose.

To kill Maria. To put an end to whatever she'd become and leave Leo to bury and mourn her all over again.

He was frozen to the spot, unable to do anything but watch as Sanda walked toward the seventh house in the street. If she found his bride in there, all of this would be over. Everything would be over.

The dog nudged his arm with her nose, clearly wanting to join in the pursuit. What the hell had he done, coming up here? Letting anyone come up here?

Panic and nausea closed his throat, and he was afraid he'd either vomit or pass out before he could manage to climb down and do something. To stop this, whatever that turned out to mean.

What he'd do afterward, how he'd possibly live with what his wife had become and with his own choices, had no space yet in his heart.

For a second, Leo thought he'd put his phone in his left pocket rather than his right where he always did. He grabbed for it just as he realized signal was non-existent so high up, and he hadn't even turned the phone on that morning.

The dog was growling again, low and deep. The woods around the village had fallen as silent as during his hike the day before. More silent than the grave.

Leo looked around, the sun and all his senses far too sharp and bright. She was here. She had to be. In the house? Seconds away from oblivion, without even the sparse comfort of his arms this time?

He lurched down off the wagon, turning at the last second to help the dog. No matter what else was happening, he didn't want her to jump and hurt herself. His body was shaking so badly he almost dropped her anyway. She twisted in his arms, then darted off after Sanda.

Leo nearly hyperventilated, his heart pounding so hard and fast he saw flashes at the edge of his sight. If he ran into the house, unarmed and shaking like a leaf, he wouldn't be able to stop Sanda no matter what he did. He probably wouldn't make it more than a few steps before he hit the ground. At least he wouldn't have to watch Maria die this time.

He staggered despite his efforts to walk slowly. Leo put a hand on the white fence around the house, ears straining to hear anything happening inside. Stereotypes and movie images flashed through his brain, too fast to make any sense.

Maria in a cartoonish casket, hands folded on her chest, helpless to resist Sanda while the sun was out. A bat with her deep green eyes, hanging under the eaves, or maybe in the cellar.

Leo grabbed the fence with both hands, leaning forward, fighting to get himself under some kind of control. His doctor wanted to write him a prescription for sedatives or an antidepressant, anything to help smooth out the pain of losing his wife. Right now, struggling to get his body moving again, he wished he had a full bottle in his pocket. That and a generous slug of the pălincă might get him through the next few minutes.

"Leo," Sanda called from inside the house.

He pushed himself upright, still trembling and fighting to catch his breath, and walked as steadily as he could across the yard. He had to try twice to get his foot up onto the low porch.

Sanda and the dog stood in the tiny living room, stripped bare of all of the cushions and tapestries that once made it a home. The room was stark white now, with odd ledges where comfortable seating used to be.

"She is not here," Sanda said, watching him closely. The dog paced from room to room, nose to the ground, hackles raised. "From the way our guide is acting, she has been. But this place is empty."

Leo opened his mouth, trying to force as much air into his body as he could.

Not here meant she was probably still alive. Not here meant she could be anywhere.

"What do you do now?" he said.

"What *we* do now is poison this ground like we did the grave," she said. "And we burn it down. I have petrol and pălincă in the wagon."

"I'll get it."

He managed not to stagger until he was back on the neatly trimmed grass. He leaned against the fence again, eyes closed, panting now that Sanda couldn't see him.

If finding out Maria was not inside and dead took this much out of him, how would he possible survive actually seeing her? Could he even stop Sanda if he tried?

He got two bottles of the alcohol and the small metal can that reeked of gas. By the time he made it back into the house, his breathing and heart had slowed to almost normal. Leo hoped Sanda didn't see how much he was sweating on such a cool morning.

"I'll use the petrol in here," she said, taking the can. "You pour the pălincă around the fence line and around the foundation of the house. It isn't as strong as pouring it into the grave, but with that and the fire, she will not return."

Leo nodded, glad for the chance to get back out when Sanda started splashing the gas around. The dog came out with him, her sensitive nose no doubt driving her away. The fumes were coating the back of his throat. He held his thumb over the mouth of the bottle to make a thin enough stream to surround the house, then the fence.

As Leo walked, he watched the other houses and the forest beyond. Sanda hadn't mentioned it, but she had to have noticed how still the birds were. Nothing moved that he could see or hear. Even the breeze had died down.

A terrible thought hit him when he'd nearly completed his circle back at the front gate. If Maria was here, if what his senses and his gut told him was right, she might be able to see him. Not only up here with a strange woman carrying weapons, but pouring booze into the ground around the house she was born in.

Leo swallowed the last few inches of the alcohol instead of completing the circle, gasping to catch his breath yet again. He couldn't go through all of this hell only to have his living wife turn away from him and never look back.

"Go back to the wagon," Sanda said. She stood in the door with a book of matches in her hand. "These old houses can go up like a torch."

Leo nodded. The dog followed him, and Sanda lit all the matches with her lighter. When she tossed them inside, he heard a thump like a huge oil furnace starting up. Sanda had closed the door before she walked away, but the curtains were already blazing.

"Will the other houses catch?" Leo said, thinking of wildfires in California.

"They may," she said. "That can't be helped. I need to move the horse upwind, but we must search the rest to be certain she's not sheltering close by."

They went though the dozen houses on either side quickly, but before they were finished, the smoke was thick and heavy throughout the village. Leo couldn't imagine the dog being able to smell anything at all with the stench.

The three of them stood with the restless horse at the edge of the forest, watching the first house burn itself out. The wagon was at the far end of the road where they'd entered. The nearby fences were burning, but so far the houses were only covered in soot.

"I have a question for you, Leo," Sanda said. She wiped at the black streaks on her face, managing to smear them instead of cleaning them off. "Where else would she shelter? Where else would she feel safe?"

Leo stared at the collapsed building where his lover was born, doing his best to keep his features neutral. He knew a place very close by where she'd feel safer even than here.

"Besides the inn? Maybe New York. Probably back in California."

"Igor will make sure the inn is protected," she said. "He'll warn her aunt and friends before he comes up here. She can't go as far as even Bucharest yet, much less get on a plane. The body is healthy, but it is weak. There must be somewhere else."

"There are other places in the US," he said. "A few in Europe. Prague, Vienna, Budapest. You just named every other place close by that I know of. "

Sanda stared at him, her red-rimmed eyes steady. Leo forced himself to keep breathing.

"We'll have to wait until the smoke clears for the dog to be able to search," she said, still watching him. "I made a mistake I hope we do not regret. I acted too soon in burning the house before we let her look for a trail."

Another wave of relief swept out from Leo's chest, making his knees weak. That combined with the mistake of underestimating how much Maria probably knew might give them the chance they needed. Sanda sighed, then coughed.

"The only place we haven't yet searched is the barn," she said. "We'll do that, then see if our guide here can pick up any scent around the outside of the village. We'll find more tools and blades in there as well."

Chapter 44

THE BARN at the edge of the village hadn't changed in Maria's lifetime, and likely not in her mother's or grandmother's. A low white stone foundation supported rough-hewn dark boards, with the highest only a foot above her head. The thick, light brown, thatched roof soared to a peak easily twice that height, the sides sharply angled to prevent snow buildup.

Maria was perfectly willing to break one of the small windows on either side of the elaborately carved wooden door. Sanda and Leo were too occupied, and still too far away, to hear such a quick noise. Instead Maria squeezed through the loose edge of the door as easily as she had when she was a teenager.

The light from those tiny windows glinted off of an orderly row of tools hanging on the far wall. Maria spotted the same blade Sanda carried, but she wanted something with more reach than that. If she was going to fight to survive with or without Leo, she wasn't going to take stupid risks now.

Rakes of various ages and designs didn't fit her needs, but an old-fashioned tool she'd used to cut down grass as a teenager sent a thrill of excitement through her aching heart. A long, curving scythe, with what looked like a new blade bright with recent sharpening, hung against the wall to her left.

Maria grasped the short wooden handles, lifting the scythe off the hooks. The wood was as old and worn as the blade was new. Probably replaced many times since the body was made. The grips fit her fingers as if they'd been carved especially for her. The Grim Reaper brought to life.

A strange low thump from the village caught her by surprise, and she stepped over to one of the windows. She couldn't see the source, but a growing orange glow needed no explanation. Sanda had lit her torch, perhaps hoping to catch Maria napping in the tiny crawlspace beneath the house like some scream queen horror movie vampire.

She wished for a cell phone of all things, or a flashlight. The walls with tools were the only parts of the barn getting any light at all. Of course if she stayed in here too long, the roof would quite likely catch a spark and give her more light than she wanted. She took down two of the long blades and three short knives. More than she could carry, but she'd be happy to cut the damned cumbersome skirt up into something practical so she could tie them around her waist.

Her small arsenal just inside the door, Maria slipped outside again. The stink of the burning house sent her recoiling back. Apparently the legendary improved sense of smell was going to be part of the bargain as time passed and her body grew stronger. She covered her nose with the end of the skirt and leaned around the edge of the barn.

Leo and a soot-covered Sanda were far closer than she expected, barely fifty paces away. The horse shifted her weight from one foot to another, clearly nervous about the fire. Or about the strigoi so close by. The dog was closer than Maria wanted, but it kept sneezing and shaking its head. The fire may very well work to her advantage after all.

Sanda turned, holding the horse's reins, and walked toward the barn. All of them were heading right toward her.

Maria froze, her mind uncharacteristically refusing to function. She couldn't get back into the woods without all of them seeing her. Sanda still carried the blade, but Maria was certain the young woman had a gun or something like it with her as well. The silver bullets were bullshit according to Magda, but a gunshot to the legs or spine would certainly erase any chance of escape. Instant healing was unfortunately bullshit as well.

She slipped back inside the barn.

Chapter 45

SANDA STEPPED onto the stone steps of the traditional wooden Romanian barn, one of the things Leo had always loved about this place. The steep angles of the heavily thatched roof matched the towering, conical hay bales scattered throughout the countryside, so much more picturesque than the square or round forms in the United States.

The air was finally clearing, and he was breathing more easily in general. Maria had eluded them so far. If he could keep Sanda from discovering the cave-like rooms in the forest barely a mile away from here, his wife would breathe for at least a few days longer.

And she'd quite likely kill a few more people along the way.

Leo leaned against the rough wooden wall. He rubbed the bruises Maria had left on his shoulder without realizing what he was doing. Sanda unlocked the door.

What were they going to do if he could get his wife away from here? Revive the tradition of Jack the Ripper, Bucharest style? Then eventually relocate to Los Angeles, maybe thin out the population of starving actors and writers?

Later. He'd have to think about that later.

"Leo, take care," Sanda said, stepping back into the doorway and reaching for her lighter. "Some of the tools are missing. She could be anywhere."

He straightened and walked toward her.

The dog barked furiously from her perch on the wagon bench.

A shadow moved inside the barn.

A blade flashed behind Sanda's knees.

An agonized shriek followed the young woman to the ground.

Leo lurched forward. Horrified for Sanda. Terrified for his wife.

Maria stepped into the doorway, dragging Sanda by the hair. Blood already soaked the wooden floor. More poured from the backs of the screaming woman's legs.

"Kill it, Leo!" Sanda shouted. "It's not your wife, kill it!"

"Yes, Leo," Maria said. "Why don't you kill it?"

She was glorious.

Maria's flesh was firm and solid, her skin rich and healthy with dark pink high in her cheeks. Her eyes glowed in the afternoon sunlight, the green deep and sparkling. Leo hadn't seen her so vibrant for years, nor so beautiful since their wedding day.

"Leo!" Sanda screamed.

"What will you do?" Maria said, her voice cold. "Sanda won't be your concern for much longer. I could cut her throat for her. I could walk away and leave her to bleed out. She won't be walking anywhere with her hamstrings sliced through."

"She's not..." Leo said.

The dog stopped barking. In the silence, Leo heard a motor at the other end of the village.

That could only be Igor.

"I will not let you or anyone else kill me," Maria said. "All that's left to decide is whether you leave with me. Make your choice, Leo."

Sanda twisted, reaching toward the blade she'd dropped.

"Move your arms again," Maria said. "And you'll lose them both."

Maria dragged Sanda aside and picked up the machete herself.

"Don't listen to it," Sanda said, panting. She grasped at Maria's hands in her hair. "This is not Maria!"

The motor was growing louder.

"What will you do?" Leo whispered. "If I go with you, what will you do?"

"No!" Sanda shrieked. The motor stopped.

Maria dropped the younger woman. She followed the body to the ground with the blade in one smooth motion.

Sanda's head rolled across the floor.

Leo's breathing, his heart, his mind, froze painfully solid. Sanda's pale blue eyes caught the sunlight—wide open and staring at nothing. Maria tried to hide it, but she stared at the spreading pool of blood soaking into the old, dry wood.

"That has to be Igor," he whispered. "He'll see the wagon."

"I know. I'll be ready for Igor. Did Sanda bring a gun or anything like that, Leo?"

"She...there's one against her stomach, in a waist holster. She was laying on it just now or..."

Maria rolled the body over and slipped the gun out. Her gaze kept straying back to the blood.

"Any others that you know of?" she said.

"In the wagon," he said.

The silence from the village below them grew louder in his ears. How long would Igor take? And far worse, would Leo help him or try to stop him now that he saw how badly his wife wanted that blood?

The dog started barking again. Leo's ability to make choices, his will, was slipping away by the second. He wasn't sure he could live with what he'd just seen. With facing more of the same for the rest of his life.

He did know he couldn't live with watching Maria die again, by Igor's hand or any other.

"Igor will hear her," Leo said. "What should I do?"

"Walk away, Leo. Go to the secret place. Don't look back, no matter what you hear. I'll come to you there."

Leo turned, his legs moving without his brain participating.

Don't watch. Don't listen.

Maybe he never had to know.

He stopped with the barn still between his body and the village.

"Maria, please," he said. "Do what you will to Igor. Don't hurt the dog."

"Then you must take her with you," Maria said. "Or she will betray me to Igor. Unless that's what you intend to do."

His wife smiled.

Cold settled into Leo's very bones.

He walked around the corner of the barn, meaning to take the dog and escape into the woods. He didn't want to know anything more. Not today. He knew more than he'd ever wanted to.

If he'd left a few minutes earlier, he would have made it.

Chapter 46

IGOR CROUCHED BEHIND THE WAGON, a pile of canvas bundles at his feet. A gleaming black handgun bigger than Leo had ever seen pointed straight at his head.

The dog must have watched Igor approaching, doing her best to make sure he knew where Maria was. Where the undead thing that so badly wanted Sanda's blood hid right this second.

"Where is Sanda?" Igor said, his voice strained and tight. "Have you found it?"

Leo's brain seemed to split then, to break into two halves that would never communicate again.

He had to save Maria.

He had to make sure she didn't get any stronger, no matter what that cost him.

A whisper of motion from the shadows behind him.

"Leo." Igor stepped forward, the massive barrel of the gun still locked on target. "Have you betrayed me? Have you betrayed us all?"

"Or will you betray me?" Maria whispered, her breath close enough to stir the hair on Leo's neck.

"Let me go, please," Leo said, not sure who he was speaking to.

He held up his hands and stepped forward. He'd seen it countless times on movie sets, but he'd never done such a thing himself. Igor kept the gun aimed at him.

"I'll take the dog and go," he said, walking toward the wagon. "I can't. Not today. Nothing else."

"Where is Sanda?" Igor said. He walked forward as Leo did, keeping the wooden frame between himself and the barn. "Did it kill her, Leo? Did you let it kill her?"

Leo staggered, barely managing to catch himself. No. That wasn't right. That wasn't fair.

He hadn't asked for any of this, or even understood what was going on around him. The side of his mind that was furious rather than terrified roared forward.

"No, Igor, *you* let this happen," he said, his voice rising. "You sent me up here instead of coming yourself! If it was so vital and important, why didn't you come up here yourself?"

Igor took several crouching steps forward until he was even with the front of the wagon.

"Go then, and go a coward," Igor said. "You're right. I never should have sent you. Sanda must have paid the price, like her grandmother and Elena did for your goddamned pride."

Leo found he didn't care what insults the man threw his way. All of it was certainly true.

Coward or not, he had no desire to die in the crossfire between Igor and his wife.

He picked up the still barking dog, relieved when she settled into growling in his arms. He kept going, aiming toward the edge of the woods not far in front of him.

"Show yourself, strigoi!" Igor shouted. "Or I will burn the barn and you with it!"

Maria laughed. The sound of it, cold and delighted, raised hard chills all over Leo's body.

He kept walking.

"Do what you think you must, Igor."

A strange whooshing noise. A burst of gunfire.

Leo crashed to the damp grass. He held the dog tight. He couldn't let her run to the noise and violence. He squeezed his eyes closed.

Don't see. Don't know.

A furious scream rang out. Maria.

Leo forced his eyes open. Igor threw a lit torch onto the thatched barn roof. Several torches on the porch and on the dry ground underneath were already at work.

The horse shrieked and reared away from the spreading flames, overturning the wagon before breaking loose and running down the hill. Igor crouched behind it. He pulled Sanda's rifle out, dropping it on top of the bundle of torches.

Igor dragged the loose wagon toward the front of the barn. He'd shoot if Maria ran for the woods. She'd burn to death in a matter of minutes.

Maria was trapped.

Chapter 47

The dwindling, rational core of Leo's mind whispered…

Just get away. Walk away.

He let the dog go, thankful when she followed the horse. Getting to his feet, Leo watched the dog's path. If he looked toward the rising light and heat behind him, he'd be lost.

And Maria would be saved.

Gunfire made him jump and nearly lose his footing. That scream again, this time agony rather than fury.

Leo fell to his knees, hands over his face.

Countless times alone in the night, he'd begged a god he didn't believe in for just one chance. One way to save her. He'd begged for more time right up until her last few days.

Then, he'd sent up whispered prayers for her last breath to be sooner rather than later.

That guilt was worse than all the rest.

He crawled forward, trying to force his legs to function. Leo managed to stagger to his feet and turn.

Igor had the rifle propped through the wagon wheel as he bent to light another torch.

The noise and heat and sharp, dry wood smell from the fire were already terrible. They were about to get far worse.

Leo took an unsteady step forward. Another.

Maria always talked about choices in recovery. How not choosing could be as dangerous as bad choices. Leo always thought he understood what she meant.

He'd had no clue until that second.

Igor ran forward and threw the torch through the barn window.

One last desperate scream forced Leo to move.

To choose.

Leo circled until he was behind Igor, hiding behind the overturned wagon again. His suitcase lay beside several bundles the older man hadn't bothered with. The first one was stiff and heavy, almost more than Leo could lift.

Inside were long iron rods. Sharpened on one end. Their purpose was as clear as it was horrifying.

He gripped one and strode forward, judging the distance as he went.

Whispers slithered through Leo's mind, intensifying with every step.

Murder.

This was murder, and he was doing it to protect a murderer.

Any emotional or moral defense became meaningless going forward.

Leo swung the iron bar at Igor's head with all of his strength.

The meaty thump of the bar against Igor's skull was nearly drowned out by the roaring fire. Igor crashed against the wagon, slumped forward, and was still.

"Maria!"

Leo ran toward the barn just as Maria vaulted out the broken window. He thought she'd fallen off of the porch until he saw the flames.

Maria rolled on the grass, batting frantically at the burning skirt. Leo grasped the fabric and pulled. As she twisted free of the heavy black garment, he caught a glimpse of dark red flesh on her pale legs.

She collided with him, taking his breath, squeezing tight enough to keep him from drawing it back in. Leo held her as well as he could with his scorched hands.

"You came back for me," she said against his ear, her voice rough and deep.

"I couldn't let him kill you."

He walked them away from the increasing heat, wishing he could stop right there and caress every inch of her. Kiss her, and claim her, and do whatever he had to so he'd never, ever lose her again.

"Let me get you some clothes," he said, veering toward the wagon. "Then we'll get away from here."

He dragged the suitcase out and opened it. When he turned back with his pajama pants, Maria crouched beside Igor. He hadn't moved.

Leo noticed then that blood mixed with the sweat and soot on his wife's face and hands. Sanda's blood. She stared at Igor now, at the deep wound Leo had made on his scalp. Maria looked up at him.

"You don't have to stay," she said. "But I can't make it far unless I feed."

Leo's mind was blank and cold, except for one thing. He had chosen. He'd learned from his wife early in her recovery how one choice, good or bad, led to another, and another, and another. He'd had his chance to either let her die again or to walk away.

He'd chosen to stay.

"I'll see if I can catch the horse," he said. "I haven't ridden in about twenty years, but she can get us a head start on anyone who tries to follow. "

Leo turned away.

Chapter 48

Two years later

THE QUIET VILLAGE hidden away in the Czech countryside was barely a mile across. A contrast to sprawling, congested Los Angeles in every way, Maria's new home transported her to an entirely new life. The two markets and handful of cafes were plenty with Leo bringing home anything else they needed from Prague. And even before the check her brother-in-law was bringing, the severing of their last ties in the United States, Leo earned more than enough for his apartment in the city and their cozy stone cottage.

Maria scrolled through her file one more time, saved her work, and exited the testing system. The bar at the bottom of the screen moved slowly from left to right, turning from red to gradually darker shades of green. Despite her confidence and hours of study, she grinned when the Passed icon lit up.

Maria Mullins, born out of her dear friend Paul's need to survive in to a culture that didn't accept him so long ago, found acceptance returning to the profession of a dead woman. This new woman thrived as much in her legal studies as she had during her short career interviewing elderly strigoi experts.

Maria herself was likely the only remaining expert in what she had become. Paul and Magda's lists—and the experts on them—had provided most of the sustenance she'd needed early in her new life. Their locations had also provided a seemingly random path that took her and Leo safely out of Romania. The only remaining person on that list, Magda, had long since forgotten her own name and everyone else's.

Maria had found no reason to suspect anyone else as young as Sanda knew anything about the strigoi. And she'd eliminated all those who'd worked together years ago to deny the family she so badly wanted with Leo.

Maria stood and stretched, groaning out loud in the empty house. These days when Leo stayed in the city were perfect for her classwork. She was surprised and gratified at how well she was doing after so many years away from studies. Maria Mullins was not quite two-thirds of the way through her qualification for the Czech bar exam without failing a single test.

She walked into the kitchen, tiny by American standards, but bright and white and cheery. Their massive kitchen in Los Angeles had mostly been wasted, with the double oven, six-burner cooktop, and what seemed like acres of counter space only necessary when they hosted some kind of party. Most of those gatherings were for either Leo's clients or hers, so caterers did all the cooking and cleanup.

This dainty, sweet space, with everything only a step or two away, suited Maria far better. She plugged in the white electric kettle and set about making herself a cup of tea. She'd been delighted to slowly regain her appetite for socially acceptable food and drink over the past few months. With the exception of pălincă, she happily indulged those appetites.

Eating the same food Leo did, admittedly with more meat than she'd wanted in the past, helped Maria avoid the terrible bouts of weakness she'd struggled with in the beginning. Once they'd settled in their new home, her supply of retired strigoi hunters depleted, Leo had nursed her almost as much as right before she'd died. She knew those days of her shaking, retching, and freezing to death from the inside as she learned her new body were the closest he'd come to madness.

Between her reinvigorated digestion and learning the patterns of this new body, she'd maintained her strength for nearly a year now. Maria wasn't quite sure if she felt better than she ever had, or if she only felt better than before she destroyed her original body.

Knowing Leo was spending the next few days with Brian made her more than a little bit lonely. She loved her brother-in-law like the sibling she'd never had. She missed him more than anyone else back in the US, with the exception of Paul.

Maria shook her head, scowling at herself for the random thoughts of ways to see Brian. No matter how she approached this fanciful meeting, there was the small matter of her dying a couple of years ago.

Thoughts of how to see Paul were not so easy to dismiss. He'd saved her life and given her a chance to reclaim her sanity. Leo opened the door by breaking his promise to follow the burial customs of her family, certainly, a vow Maria was eternally thankful he'd ignored. Paul and Magda gave her the knowledge of how to survive past the first few hours.

Of course when it came to anyone from her life in Romania, there was the added challenge of explaining the rash of deaths right after her funeral, then Leo's disappearance. They'd both kept a watch on Interpol for the first several months, but never found mention of either of their names. She was sure Leo still checked from time to time, especially as his involvement in the European movie and TV industry grew. Still, nothing.

She walked back out to the living room, barely large enough for a sofa and three chairs, and curled up on the sofa.

Maria had no intention of letting Magda waste away, alone, forgetting, forgotten. She'd never take the older woman's blood for many reasons. But she'd also never lost her ability to drain energy, even as her need for that sort of nourishment waned along with the need for blood.

Less than an hour with Magda would give Maria the chance to repay her for so many hours of vital information. The former party boss made it clear on those early visits how distasteful she found the idea of her mind dwindling away, and certainly of being dependent upon others for changing her diapers and bathing her.

Stubborn family members refusing to allow Magda the relief of the EU's assisted suicide laws would not stand in Maria's way.

Her mind worked through the calculations in a matter of seconds, even though she had plenty of time before she needed to kill again. Draining Magda, bringing her the gift of compassion, would let Maria put that need off for another couple of months, well into the new year. She and Leo could live normal lives until the spring.

Well, not exactly normal.

She took her empty cup into the kitchen, grabbed a light jacket, and headed out for her afternoon walk. Moving always calmed her racing thoughts and anxieties. Thinking of that horrible word did just the opposite.

Normal may be getting back to her own work, with the easy adjustment of helping writers with international contracts. Maria had never been one to sit at home while someone else had an energetic life and career. Online communications and her European legal credentials as a brand new person would solve her identity problems before they ever started.

Normal was not forcing her husband and her to live separate lives, each secret from the other. His stays in Prague or elsewhere in Europe gave her the privacy she needed for her body's demands. Those stays also gave Leo his choice of not knowing or understanding those demands.

But it hurt to be hidden, nonexistent to the outside world. Only people in this village knew who she was now, and that she and Leo were together.

Maria waved to those neighbors, but she walked quickly toward the forest. They were all safe from her less and less frequent needs for anything but company, as they always had been. Maria's deeper needs were safely met elsewhere. But chatting and company never suited her when her thoughts took this turn.

Leo's refusal to talk about starting the family they'd been denied in her first life was moving from annoying to upsetting. She had no reason to doubt Magda's insistence that strigoi could reproduce after three years, not the seven years of legend. She also had no reason to tell

Leo the time frame he'd surely found looking into the folklore for himself was so inaccurate.

What had all of this been for if not that? The fact that her husband asked damned good questions about how they'd deal with the destinies of those children, their strigoi fate, didn't help her temper or the conversations.

How the hell did anyone deal with uncertainty when it came to their children? They could have diseases or disorders no one suspected. They could turn out to be serial killers, the indiscriminate kind. Or they could simply be miserable, cruel people no matter how hard their parents tried to do the right thing.

There were more ways to screw it up than there were to get it right. Even if spawning a new line of strigoi wasn't on the list of things to worry about.

She was nowhere near ready to give up on that dream.

Maria waited for a few cars to pass on the motorway before she finally entered the woods. The dirt path was carefully maintained, and hardly anyone was out here in the early winter. She loved the calm and quiet, with hardly any animals to fall silent as she passed or flee before her.

She so badly wanted to talk all of this over with someone she trusted, someone besides Leo with all of his caution. Paul would be ideal for reasons growing too good to ignore.

Maria had a suspicion he wouldn't be overly shocked at hearing from her. The borderline illegal research he'd done into Magda's life covered more than her past with the Communist Party and her mental deterioration. Before she'd become one, Paul knew as much about strigoi as Maria did.

Paul was also the only person she trusted besides Leo. Maria's heart broke when she thought of Ana, but her childhood friend's fears ran too deep. Anyone in that village, or in all of Transylvania, knowing about her was far too risky.

She'd trust Paul with her life, old or new, and she knew in her bones he would never betray that trust. And if any person on the face of the earth besides Leo would accept her return, likely even celebrate it, Paul would be the one.

A slow smile curved Maria's lips. She wouldn't have to bother with cloak and dagger tactics, at least not beyond a private email account. She was studying to get herself back into business working with writers, after all. And Paul was the best writer she knew. Successful as he was, he'd be as eager as anyone else to improve his connections and his bargaining power in the fast-growing European market.

Thanks to his rabid curiosity and obsessive attention to details while working with Maria, Paul didn't depend on his agent to make such arrangements anymore. The whole thing would be absurdly easy. And talking with her dear friend, maybe even seeing him in person, would be well worth the risks.

Chapter 49

The historic center of Prague contrasted with downtown LA, and anywhere else in the United States, more than enough to still delight Leo. So many of the trends and affectations of Southern California had been a way of life here for centuries. The tall curved windows looked out not over a gridlocked highway packed with gleaming metal boxes, but over lovely stone buildings, the elaborate facades painted a dozen bright colors. Locals and tourists alike strolled along the twisting cobblestone streets, in and out of shops and cafes, chatting and enjoying each other's company.

Leo accomplished every bit as much working here as he ever had back in the US. In fact, he was busier than he ever had been. The difference was he enjoyed every second of his working life a thousand times more.

He glanced at his calendar, more a habit than a necessity here, and definitely today. Nothing was on his schedule other than waiting here for his brother to arrive. The entire office, converted from an old apartment building many years ago and upgraded for the demands of modern movies and TV over the past several months, was empty except for him and the security guards.

A soft chime, part of those modern upgrades, let Leo know

someone had arrived downstairs. He touched his monitor and answered in Czech, another of his recent acquisitions.

"This is Leo."

"Good morning, sir. A large truck has arrived from the airport, wanting to unload here. Your brother arrived with it. Shall I send them to the prop storage warehouse?"

"Those are mostly records," Leo said. "A couple of crates should be marked personal. Those go to my apartment. The rest to the data warehouse. Please send Brian up, and two coffees. Thanks, Jan."

Leo looked down three stories to the street level. A white Skoda cargo truck, big for old European city standards, was just pulling away from the curb. He smiled, wondering what kind of havoc a typical American tractor trailer would create trying to navigate these twisty passages where pedestrians were the rule, not the exception.

He crossed the room, shoes tapping on the richly aged hardwood, and opened the door. Brian jumped back, lowering his hand.

"Couldn't let me knock, could you?"

Leo pulled his brother into a hug so hard the younger man grunted. Two years was too damned long. The guard's assistant grinned as he walked by to put the ceramic and silver coffee service on a low table.

"Much more fun this way," Leo said. The assistant closed the door, and they both sat on a curved, wood framed sofa. The deep burgundy velvet set with two chairs and a footstool had survived the renovations at Leo's insistence. "Good flight?"

"Yeah, great flight," Brian said. "Slept like a log this time. Seems a shame to waste that fancy business class seat when I'm snoring and drooling the whole way."

"Worth every penny," Leo said. "I made that flight more than enough times in coach to never want to repeat the experience. Did customs hassle you with all the cargo?"

"Nope, not a word. They said everything was arranged and in order. They didn't even check my bags. What kind of pull do you have around here, brother?"

Leo handed a flowery cup to Brian.

"You might want extra milk in that," he said, picking up his own.

"Way stronger than back home. I don't have much pull at all. The local authorities are pretty happy with the money we bring in with our little projects, though."

"Not that different than the US, then." Brian sipped, grimaced, and picked up the silver creamer. "Tax credits falling from the sky. Does all this include a place for you to live?"

"Yeah, just a couple of blocks away," Leo said. He wasn't about to tell Brian about his other home. "Not far off the old town square. It can get a bit noisy at night, but it's a good scene. The guards probably already have your bags over there. Got something for me to sign?"

Brian picked up his gleaming black briefcase. It looked more like a mobile bank vault than the Old World leather and brass versions Leo saw on the street every day. Fingerprint ID built into the glossy surface completed the modern spy experience, every bit as well as any of his friend Paul's thrillers did.

"Customs didn't even bat an eye at this," Brian said, pulling out a thick blue folder. "Gave me palpitations carrying the damned thing around, though. I don't see how you sign checks bigger than this every day without losing your shit."

Leo expected two and a half million dollars or so for liquidation of all of their US assets—the house, cars, his firm, investments, as well as Maria's firm and life insurance. The check was for 3.4 million. Leo raised his eyebrows and looked at his brother.

"What happened?"

Brian grinned. "My real estate woman and my broker worked a little bit of magic on the commissions. If you're going to stay all the way over here, you need all the cushion you can get. That reminds me, Mom and Dad. Wish they could make it, miss you, same as always."

"Well, be sure to thank your people for me," Leo said. He signed the proof of receipt and handed it back to Brian. "Help me pick out gifts while you're here? For Mom and Dad too, I suppose."

Brian watched Leo for several seconds.

"You look good, Leo," he said, smiling. "You look strong, healthy again. Corporate hair and all."

Leo ran a hand over his head, still surprised at his own spiky hair. He'd gained quite a bit of grey scattered throughout that caught the light, but he didn't look much different than he had back in the States otherwise.

"Yeah, I just cut it," he said. "I'm still using too much shampoo in the shower. I kinda miss having a mop like yours."

"Listen, how long are you staying?" Brian said. "People besides our parents are starting to ask."

Leo stared at the floor and smiled. Uncomfortable as it was, he'd gotten used to the strange, liquid shift in his mind, like water moving between layers of heavy plastic. After so many weeks and months, he rarely remembered to wish it would stop. He never expected it to anymore.

"To tell you the truth, I don't see any reason to go back," he said. This part was the truth. "We were always either sending someone out here to manage shoots or scrambling for a translator or help with work visas. I've been able to put together a team to handle all of that. Expenses are still a fraction of what we'd pay in the California. Cost of living, too."

"You don't get homesick?" Brian said, leaning back and kicking his loafers off. "Not even a little bit?"

"I miss you. I'd love to meet this woman who's agreed to marry you for some reason. A few friends, but they want to visit." Leo steeled himself for the lie to his own brother. "The one I miss most isn't back in the States or anywhere else. I don't know why, but that's easier to take here than it would be back there. Maybe for the holidays. Of if you ever set the date for your wedding."

"You'll be there for the wedding if I have to drug you and ship you under the plane," Brian said. "I'm happy to visit, especially if someone springs for that first-class transit. I hope this isn't too strange to ask, but do you ever get back to Transylvania? That was a rough time, but I liked it there."

Leo's mind shifted again, this time hard enough to force his stomach into a slow roll. His last few weeks in Romania had been enough to last this lifetime and a few more besides.

They'd have to be. He could never go back there again. Alone or not, the risk was too great.

"Don't know if I'll ever be able to manage that, little brother. I love it there too. I think the good memories would make going back even worse."

"That reminds me," Brian said, digging back into his high tech briefcase. He handed Leo several folders in different colors, each with the logo of a fertility clinic on the front. "All taken care of."

Leo nodded, chewing on his lip to keep his face from reflecting his feelings. No matter how he thought about it or tried to figure things out, on his own or with Maria, her decline had started with this. Months stretching into years, full of hope and disappointment. The cycles higher and deeper every time, and harder to recover from.

No matter what the final catalyst had been, their decision to try to have a baby had led to the end. To his decidedly odd dual lifestyle.

And his dual mind.

"Thank you for this, Brian. Any problems?"

"Not really. Once they saw the power of attorney and everything in order, they were very kind and efficient." He scowled for a second. "The only weird thing was someone else had been in touch before me. At three different places."

The shift in Leo's mind was more of a dislocation this time, threatening to join what he worked so hard to keep separate. He closed his eyes for a second until it subsided.

"Before you?" he said.

"Yeah," Brian said. "They couldn't tell me much, just that someone else had asked about your stored...belongings. I think they suspected it was me. Whoever it was didn't get far, of course. They were just as careful to check for authorization as they were with me, and this person didn't have it."

"Did they say who it was?"

Brian shook his head. "Nope. Just a person. Typical routine of protecting the one trying to do something strange instead of the one it's being done to. Any idea who the hell would be wanting to mess with that?"

Leo leaned forward to pour more coffee, using the excuse to hide his face. He knew. There was only one person it could have been.

"No idea," he said. "I guess we were both just well known enough to attract weirdoes. Sad, third-rate weirdoes who weren't ambitious enough to go after a writer or movie star. Pretty lazy if you ask me."

"That's one way to look at it," Brian said, adding cream to his second cup. "Well, all of it's destroyed now, so no more worries about that. Does it bother you? Letting that part of her go?"

Leo sighed, looking out the window at the second-hand clothing shop across the street. The only thing that bothered him was knowing his wife had tried to go behind his back in such a way.

"It makes me sad, sure," Leo said. "But I can't imagine trying to raise a kid on my own. I've been thinking about getting the snip, actually. May as well."

"I know you aren't quite ready to think about this." Brian ran one hand across his chin, then looked into Leo's eyes. "I hope I don't sound like an asshole for bringing it up. You may meet someone, Leo. If I can get engaged to a woman miles out of my league despite everyone's low expectations, you may not want to write that off entirely."

Leo snorted, trying not to let laughter surge up and run away with him. His real reasons for considering a vasectomy would have to stay inside his own slowly breaking mind. Even if those reasons were driving wedges to push the fractures deeper.

"I'm getting too old for that nonsense," he said. "Even if I decide to date again someday, that's not the best kind of surprise for your late forties."

"Oh yeah, you're positively ancient," Brian said, laughing. "You do remember our grandfather was famously into his fifties by the time Mom was born, right? You might not be ready to pack it in and throw away the key just yet. You never know, brother. You never know."

EPILOGUE

MARIA WALKED SLOWLY down the cobblestone street of Magda's last earthly home, losing herself in the perfectly curated and arranged fantasy. Almost everyone nodded or smiled at her as she passed by.

She tried to push the similarities to Prague out of her mind. Much as she treasured her memories of walking those narrow, winding streets with Leo years ago, she resented the fact that they could never be there together now. Even so far from all their family and friends, being seen in the city with her own husband created far too much risk of being recognized. The only person who truly knew her here in Austria no longer remembered anything she'd once known.

She'd stopped by the coffee shop for one of their wonderful espressos as she always did. Magda hadn't met her there for a long time. Magda didn't meet anyone any more. Her mind had retreated permanently more than a year ago. Maria hoped it was into a happy past rather than into empty oblivion. Or fear.

She was heading toward two neat shops with dark wooden fittings and painted signs on the windows—accurate and charming pre-World War examples of a doctor's office and a pharmacy. Erick the barista told her the residents often self-diagnosed their problems before the doctors had a chance to, taking themselves to trusted experts. Many of them also remembered they could go there to visit friends who were too ill to remain in their apartments. Both buildings connected to the wings for the most severe dementia patients.

Maria could have easily gone through a different entrance on the other side of the complex, straight into the nursing facility rather than through the assisted living area. Her first visit that way, nearly a year ago after Magda's final transfer, had been too damned depressing. At least this way she had the fantasy before the brutal reality.

She hated to imagine Leo having to visit her in that awful hospice ward, walking alone through the unflinching truth of her first death.

Maria visited less frequently since Magda's steep decline, waiting for the right time to act. The flashes of clarity had been brief for the first few months. As long as they happened at all, she waited. The last time Maria visited, everyone told her it had been weeks since Magda knew anyone. Or anything. She hadn't been out of her room in a few months.

Today would be their last visit.

And she'd continue on to Budapest for her first visit with Paul. Her suspicions about his lack of shock, or even surprise, when she contacted him had proven delightfully true.

The charming brass bell tinkled over her head when she opened the doctor's office door. Several people sitting in the waiting room glanced at her and smiled before going back to their books or newspapers. No blaring televisions disrupted the strangely peaceful space. A middle-aged woman behind the desk nodded. Apparently the youthful appearance desired for the shops and cafes was not deemed appropriate here.

"Good to see you, Mrs. Leiber," Maria said in German. She hadn't spoken Romanian here or anywhere else for years. Today might prove to be the last time for even longer, assuming Magda remembered any language at all.

"Mrs. Mullins," the older woman said. "Always such a pleasure."

She stood and kissed each of Maria's cheeks, then squeezed her hands before sitting behind the desk again. No one ever noticed the slight coolness of her flesh any more, not even when she was so close to feeding.

"How's Magda doing today?"

Mrs. Leiber smiled sadly and closed her eyes for a second.

"I'm afraid she's continuing to decline. She hasn't truly been conscious for a few weeks now. I know your visits help her, though." Mrs. Leiber's pale blue eyes and mouth drew down in a scowl. "No one in her family has bothered for years now."

"She's been so dear to me for so long," Maria said. "I'm happy to bring her even a small bit of comfort."

"That you do." Mrs. Leiber touched a button hidden under the desk, and the pale wooden door to her right clicked open. "The code hasn't changed since you last visited."

Mrs. Leiber turned back toward her computer monitor, then grabbed a small purple envelope leaning against the keyboard. Unfamiliar handwriting addressed it to Mrs. Maria Mullins.

"I almost forgot," she said. "This is for you. A courier brought it a few minutes before you arrived."

Maria tried to hide her surprise and pleasure, most inappropriate with the reason for her visit. No one but Paul could have sent this in advance of their long-planned reunion in the City of Light. No one besides him knew Maria Mullins had once been Maria Sabov, or that either had ever traveled to this idyllic valley in Austria.

"Thank you, Mrs. Leiber. From another dear friend."

She decided to wait until she left Magda's room to read Paul's note. How often and how easily Maria had killed wouldn't make any difference today. This would not be an easy visit.

She slipped the envelope into her purse and walked through the antiseptic pale blue hallway, far more like the one in the hospice ward where she herself had died than she realized.

Maria wouldn't have recognized the woman in the narrow hospital bed without the room number to guide her. Magda's wispy, white hair floated on the pillow, her puffy face and wasted body nearly impossible to reconcile with the strong woman Maria walked through the retirement community with so many times. An IV Maria knew Magda would have refused if she'd been able ran into the thin flesh of her wrist. Evidence of her family's interference despite their refusal to visit.

In the end, Magda passed away more gently than falling into sleep. Maria touched her temple and her heart. The remaining life force lifted away, light as dandelions puffed by a warm spring breeze. Her wasted chest fell and did not rise again.

That warmth moved through Maria just as easily, heightening her senses and sensations. Low conversations in the hallway, the faint scent of Magda's emptying bladder, the cold metal bedrail against her hip. Even such long-used and faint energy would sustain Maria for weeks.

"Thank you for saving my life, Magda," Maria whispered in Romanian. She gently closed the staring brown eyes. Tears stood in her own. "Calm and peaceful journey into the next one."

Maria sat in a reclining chair beside the bed, not wanting to leave the room so quickly after she'd arrived. She'd always stayed fifteen minutes once Magda moved to this intensive care section, even if the older woman was sleeping. No need to interrupt her routine on this day. The European efficiency of the staff assured her of at least twenty-five more minutes before anyone entered the room.

And even if someone came in sooner, no one would ever suspect her of such gentle assistance with no sign of a struggle or any sort of trauma. Maria was quite certain whoever discovered Magda had passed on would be as relieved as she herself was.

She had no illusions of ever being able to repay Magda for so many gifts of information, of courage, of survival. Her one small act of compassion, so unlike killing for revenge or even sustenance, would have to suffice.

Not wanting to sink into sadness over Magda's death or melancholy over Leo's first trip back to the US without her, Maria turned her thoughts to her reunion with Paul the next morning. She opened the purple envelope, hoping he hadn't been delayed in his travels.

Maria's newly invigorated blood ran cold and sluggish before she read to the end of the sprawling Romanian script.

My dear Maria,

I trust you've stopped in Austria to bring poor Magda's life to a graceful end. She deserves that much, no matter how badly she betrayed me and everyone else who has fallen victim to you and your unnatural appetites. And to mine.

Do not fear for your friend Paul, or for your lovely vacation in Budapest. And do not worry for Leo and his time at his brother's wedding in the United States. You and I must meet, but we have no need to involve others.

I will contact you after you return to your village and Leo returns to his work in Prague.

This will be settled between the two of us alone.

Yours in this new life,

Igor

ABOUT KARI

Kari Kilgore's wanderlust and imagination lead her all over the world on grand adventures. Her heart and family bring her home to her native Appalachian Mountains of Virginia. From that solid base, she and her husband Jason A. Adams bring those adventures to life in fiction.

Kari writes science fiction, fantasy, horror, and contemporary fiction, and she's happiest when she surprises herself. She lives at the end of a long dirt road in the middle of the woods with Jason, various house critters, and wildlife they're better off not knowing more about.

The Confidential Adventure Club

For Kari's exclusive free After The End stories and deleted scenes, discounts, early pre-sale releases, adorable pet photos, and a whole lot more not available anywhere else, visit The Confidential Adventure Club at www.smarturl.it/c-a-club.

Hope to see you there!

www.karikilgore.com
www.spiralpublishing.net

ALSO BY KARI KILGORE

I hope you enjoyed reading *Until Death* as much as I enjoyed writing it. For news about the upcoming sequel and to check out more of my fiction, head over to www.karikilgore.com.

The Confidential Adventure Club

Want more fiction from Kari, including stories, discounts, and box sets not available anywhere else? Want to hear about locations, research, and other cool things that inspired this story and beyond? All that and adorable pet photos, too?

Join The Confidential Adventure Club and get a thank you gift of a free short story and a whole lot more at www.smarturl.it/c-a-club.

Hope to see you there!

Novels:

The Dream Thief

Dreaming the Storm: Book One of the Storms of Future Past Series

Joining the Storm: Book Two of the Storms of Future Past Series

Fighting the Storm: Book Four of the Storms of Future Past Series

Novellas:

Songs in the Mountain

Legacy of the Land

Restricted Species

The Becalmed

In the Pines

Into the Storm: Book Three of the Storms of Future Past Series

Short Stories:

Renovations

Intentions

The Garbage Belt

The Seeds of Love

Wicked Bone

The Sound of Murder

Terminalia

Little Five: A Terminalia Story

Reflections

Collections:

Fantastic Women: A Dark Fantasy Novella Trio

Fantastic Shorts: Volume 1 - A Fantasy Short Story Collection

"Kari Kilgore is an author to watch—her lyrical voice a siren song; her insight, conjured voodoo."

—Richard Thomas, author of *Breaker* and *Tribulations*